ISBN: 978-0-9945886-0-9

First published in Australia in 2016 by Kylie Chan
More information: http://www.kyliechan.com

Typeset in 10pt Sabon Lt Standard
Cover design by Madeleine Chan
Printed and Distributed by Lightning Source (Ingram)

The Bride With Red Hair

Kylie Chan

This novella was created as part of a Master of Philosophy in Creative Writing at the University of Queensland.

Dr Kim Wilkins of UQ was profoundly instrumental in making this novella possible, and making it as good as it could possibly be.

1921

The demon drove the stolen truck up the long drive, surrounded by bamboo, to the white-painted steel gates of the White Tiger's stables. The sun was rising over the centre of the city of Shanghai twenty kilometres away, painting the sky on the horizon hues of pink and lilac. Lai stepped out and spoke to the gatekeeper who was in a traditional black jacket and pants with toggles and loops.

'I'm Hong Lai, I'm the shipping agent, here to collect the horses.'

The servant quickly opened the gates for her. 'Yes, Miss Hong. Go through and around the back of the building; the Master and the horses are there.'

The demon drove the truck through the gates and past the long brick stable block, and stopped in the courtyard behind. Lai stepped out of the truck onto cobblestones strewn with straw overflowing from the stables, and walked up to the White Tiger. The tight-fitting gold silk cheongsam she'd chosen to wear today was obviously working; he admired her openly, his eyes roaming her slim, athletic figure from the toes of her silk shoes to her flaming red bob. She tossed her hair, letting the curls speak their own language, and his appreciation obviously deepened. The grooms standing behind him, holding the fine racehorses, smiled slightly to themselves – they knew their father's weakness.

The Tiger was in human form, a tall, muscular man in his mid-thirties, the thick white sideburns that framed his face hinting at his true nature. His outfit of fashionable cream linen suit with a gold silk cravat and a genuine panama hat must have cost a fortune from one of the high-end tailors in the city. The grooms wore modern Western garb as well – shirts and trousers. The whole effect was of a progressive Chinese business dealing in fine horse flesh. The spindle-legged mares behind the Tiger stood motionless with only their flicking ears showing their unease.

Lai strode up to the Tiger, embracing him and kissing him on both cheeks and then remaining close to whisper into his ear.

'When the horses are delivered I would love to return to Shanghai and talk more about my transport business.'

1

She squeezed his hard biceps to make the point, then stepped back, still smiling.

He grinned broadly, showing his extended canines. 'I look forward to it.'

She nodded to him, then guided the grooms to lead the horses to the truck, the Tiger following.

'You have the money?' she asked the Tiger as her demon driver opened the truck.

The Tiger stared at her driver. The demon was in his True Form: black and scaly, with bulging red eyes and tusks. 'Where did you get a tame demon that big? He's huge.'

'He was a gift from my last husband,' she said.

'Doesn't he have a human form? Normal humans may see him.'

'Are you worried that he will spook the horses?' she said.

He harrumphed. 'Of course not. My horses are the best in the world; *nothing* scares them. But there are rules about humans seeing us in our True Forms.'

She shrugged. 'He doesn't have a human form, and I'll drive the truck myself to the dock to ensure that the horses are safely loaded onto the steamship.'

The Tiger was correct; the horses walked meekly past the demon, up the ramp and into the truck. The demon rattled the bars as he secured the animals and closed the tailgate.

The Tiger handed her a large piece of paper with official-looking writing on it. 'Thirty-four thousand yuan, as agreed. I'll pay the rest when the mares are delivered safely. This note is good anywhere in the world, it's from one of the new international banks in Hong Kong.'

She nodded to him; Celestials could always be trusted to pay their dues, particularly Celestials as highly-ranked as him. 'I hope this is the beginning of a successful partnership for both of us. I'll wire you as soon as the horses arrive safely in Ireland.'

'Oh, I hope so too, Miss Hong,' the Tiger said, eyeing her appreciatively again. 'I've never had a fox wife before, I would love to see more of you.'

'And I would love to see more of you,' she said, and embraced him again just for good measure. She waved and entered the passenger side of the truck.

As soon as they were out the gates of the Tiger's estate, Lai slipped the bank draft into her leather choker and breathed a sigh of relief.

'Excellent job, Miss Hong,' the demon said. 'I'll have your payment when we reach the ship.'

Lai leaned on the window to watch the busy traffic, most of it horse- or human-drawn; motor cars and trucks were a rarity. Two-storey wooden shophouses lined the street, the pillars holding up their balconies and projecting roofs adorned with company names in large calligraphy. A trishaw driver pulled his vehicle – a heavy-duty bicycle converted into a small cart – to the side of the road under an awning, and grimaced at them as they rolled past. There was only just enough room for the truck on the narrow road and, as they bounced over the gravel and potholes, pedestrians leaped under the shop awnings.

'You were right,' she said. 'The horses never made a peep. Your appearance didn't worry them at all.'

The demon grunted. 'One day I will find the Mother who took my human form and make her *suffer*.'

'I'm sure you will,' Lai said, and closed her eyes to nap while the truck rumbled over the bumpy road towards the Shanghai docks.

The truck stopped at the docks and she jumped awake. The sun was higher in the sky, making the filthy water between the cargo ships glitter as if it was clean. She stepped out to watch as the demon unloaded the horses and carefully led them up the enclosed ramp and into the hands of another demon, this time in human form, waiting for them on the ship. The demon came back down the ramp and she quivered with excitement; she was being paid *twice* for this.

The ship's engines surged to life and a gush of foul-smelling coal smoke erupted from the smoke stack. A demon dock worker released the moorings and the ship moved slowly, then picked up speed and headed down the river towards the sea.

The ship chugged around the turn of the river and headed out to sea unchallenged, and Lai released a breath she hadn't realised she'd been holding.

The demon sauntered up to her and grinned. 'Will silver ingots do for payment? The Westerners pay for the opium with silver.'

'Of course,' Lai said. 'We agreed on ten thousand yuan for each horse – that's thirty thousand.'

The demon waved one hand over its shoulder and three smaller demons – all with scales and tusks, like their master – strode out of a nearby warehouse. One passed the demon a lumpy canvas satchel, clinking with metal, and he handed it to her. She opened it and checked inside – it contained at least a dozen one-catty silver ingots, each shaped like a small boat.

'Thank you for your excellent service,' the demon said. 'How do I contact you again for our next transaction?'

'There won't be one,' she said. 'This is it for me. No more, I'm tired of this life. This,' she raised the satchel, 'will start me on a new, honest path. I might study something worthwhile, that will help people, like medicine.'

'Terrible waste of your skills and intelligence,' the demon said. 'Are you sure?'

She opened her mouth to reply, but the Tiger materialised in human form behind the boss demon and swiftly removed his head with a gold sword, making the demon explode into black streamers of demon essence. In less than a second the Tiger despatched all the demons, then turned to her and snarled.

She stood her ground. 'You're a Celestial! You can't hurt me, I'm not a demon. All of you Celestials are sworn to protect us!'

His face went slack and he lowered the sword. 'That's right. We only destroy demons, we're sworn to protect all humans.' He raised his sword again, and his face became more tiger than man. 'But you're not human, Lai, you're a fox Shen and you're a *thief*!'

Lai dropped the silver, changed to fox form, and ran. She scooted beneath the truck, ran to a pile of boxes held in large nets and dodged quickly through them, using all her fox agility. She hit a dead-end, took a deep breath, and scurried up the walls of the stacked tea chests, aromatic with black tea, to the top of the pile. She took a moment to look around.

'Don't run, I want to talk to you!' the Tiger shouted. 'Where the *fuck* are my goddamn *horses*?'

She dodged around tea chests and under opium bales, and didn't stop until she was sagging with exhaustion. She hunched down and slinked through the cargo stacked on the docks until she found a ship based in Hong Kong and clambered over the mooring rope to hide on board. She grimaced, her whiskers twitching, as she leaped down from the deck into the hold, ripe with the sweet smell of opium. She hated the taste of rat, but there were plenty of them in the hold to keep her fed on the three-day trip to Hong Kong.

She quickly changed to human and checked the leather choker; the oil impregnating the leather had kept the cheque dry, and it was one of the new promissory notes, good, as he had said, in any city in the world. She breathed a sigh of relief; she could still follow her heart and live a new life in a new city, help people, build some good karma, settle down, have a family. She changed back to fox form and buried her head under her paws. She was so tired of this life. She sighed again, her red fur rippling, and pulled her three white-tipped tails around to cover her nose. Definitely changing her life. Enough was enough.

'There he is,' Mei said from the front passenger seat.

Her brother twisted behind the wheel to catch a glimpse of her boss. 'Where? Where?'

'Which one is he?' Mei's mother said from the back seat. 'I can't see anything. Lean back, Old Bean.'

Mei's father grunted in the passenger seat behind her. 'I'm leaning back as far as I can!'

'He's in front of the doors,' Mei said

Tony didn't see them. He entered the building's spacious glass-walled lobby, disappearing into the morning office crowd.

'He went in. He was the good-looking one –'

'Oh the *good-looking* one,' Mei's father said.

'In the suit...' Mei's voice trailed off as she realised that all the men wore suits. She shrugged. 'I'd better go, I'll be late.' She nodded to her brother. 'I'll make my own way home, you don't need to pick me up.'

'No staying late again,' her father said sternly. 'Be home in time for dinner.'

Mei opened the car door and grabbed her leather briefcase. 'I'll do my best, but some of the figures aren't adding up.'

'Leave the figures and come home to your family!' Ba Ba said.

'Hurry up, I have to be in Sai Kung in thirty,' Mei's brother said. 'And I still have to drop the oldies off at their practice.'

'Oldies!' Ba Ba said.

'Drive carefully, Di Di,' she said.

He waved as she closed the door, and pulled away from the kerb to take her parents to her mother's medical practice, and then to drive himself to his intern year at the veterinary surgery. She turned and looked up at the office building; it was a modern skyscraper with the luxury of landscaped gardens around it, and a glossy ground floor lobby with multiple lifts for the different floors. She smiled and joined the other smartly-dressed office workers walking with purpose to their high-powered careers.

Mei tried to ignore Sandy's tuneless humming in the next cubicle as she glared at the computer. She'd spent the last two days going over the monthly figures again and again – Sandy had helped her this third time – and still had no idea where the money had gone. Nothing for it. She printed out the summary, retied her long red hair into a neat bun, and rose. Time to face the music.

She picked the printouts up at the printer and walked to the Chief Financial Officer's office. She passed the beige-screened cubicles of her fellow officer workers, her feet soft on the new carpet that had just been laid. She'd never had a boss who looked after his staff so well; their office environment was spacious, light-filled and modern, with clean new furniture and the latest equipment. She tapped on the CFO's door.

'Enter,' Kwok Kam said from inside.

She opened the door and went in. Kwok was studying his computer, and he scowled at her. His thin face was full of malice under his spiky shock of grey hair; he'd made it clear many times that he didn't like being disturbed. The rest of the staff speculated that he spent all his time hiding in his office looking at porn and avoiding work, and they had given him the nickname 'Nasty Kwok'.

'Well?' he said after a couple of uncomfortable minutes.

Mei gathered herself and put the paper on the desk. 'I've consolidated the accounts for the last month and two hundred and forty-four thousand Hong Kong dollars are missing from the Hong Kong side of the company. There's no matching expenditure anywhere.'

His scowl deepened. 'Did you check the figures?'

'Three times.'

'Did ask someone to help you?'

'Sandy helped me.'

'Sandy. Heh.' He snatched the papers from the table and glared at them. He angrily flipped the pages, then pushed them at her. 'Ask Tony.' His scowl turned into a sneer. 'Go right ahead and tell the owner of the company that you lost nearly a quarter of a million dollars.'

'I was hoping you'd have an idea where it went,' she said, hearing her voice squeak.

He tossed the paper on the desk and turned back to his computer. 'That's your job.' He waved her away. 'Go. Show Tony this. I'm sure he'll be thrilled.'

Her heart sank and she made her way to the executive side of the company. All the lower-level staff had to pass through Reception, and be buzzed through a locked door into the executive section – a standard procedure in Hong Kong companies, where the bosses' privacy was of paramount importance. She stopped and smiled at the receptionist, desperately hoping that Tony wasn't there and she didn't need to explain why so much money was missing. She loved visiting with the boss, and enjoyed spending time with Tony, but she didn't want to go to him to explain how she'd lost him – and his company – so much money. She wanted him to see her as competent, intelligent … and attractive.

'Is Mr Wong in? I need to see him,' she said.

'Just a minute, Mei,' the receptionist said, and called Tony. She told him Mei was there, and nodded. 'He'll see you.' She pressed the button under the desk to open the door, and Mei went through.

The executive side of the of company wasn't much different from the admin side – same plush carpet, same beige walls – but the executive offices were enormous. What was more striking was the strange, acrid smell that filled this side of the floor, a combination of burnt rubber and melted plastic, with a note of sewage. Mei had asked other staff about it, and nobody else had noticed it. It was probably only Mei's more sensitive nose that detected it. Tony's office was on the corner, with his secretary sitting at a desk larger than Mei's outside it. Mei approached her and smiled through the discomfort. She opened her mouth to say something and Tony's door flew open, making her jump.

'Just the woman I wanted to see,' Tony said. 'Come on in.'

Mei gripped the pages holding the figures and slinked into his wood-panelled office, as large as four sets of cubicles on the other side of the floor. One wall was floor-to-ceiling windows, overlooking Hong Kong harbour. A set of rosewood bookshelves covering the back wall held a display of all the gifts Tony had been given by fellow company directors when he attended their banquets and conferences: engraved plates, small glass sculptures, and a couple of miniature cars and sailboats.

Tony threw himself into his leather executive chair and she sat across from him.

'You look concerned,' he said. 'How many times do I have to tell you that it's all right if the numbers don't add up, just come and ask me? You worry too much.'

Mei deflated. He was right, he was always telling her that. 'I don't like bothering you, Mr Wong. I'm an accountant, I should be handling it.'

'Tony, please, Mei, we've known each other for two years now.'

He leaned on the desk and clasped his hands together. He smiled, revealing disarming dimples on his cheeks that Mei found completely entrancing. Tony was in his early thirties, young to be in charge of such a large company, and one of the most eligible bachelors in Hong Kong. Mei was intensely aware of his dark, charismatic aura as she sat across from him, and when he studied her with that intense look on his face, she could only wonder what he would be like in a more ... casual setting. He stirred feelings inside her that were extremely unprofessional and totally inappropriate, particularly considering that she was just an accountant and he was a wealthy entrepreneur. But she could still dream, and she often did – of spending her evenings out at the social occasions on the arm of this extremely handsome and available –

'So what's the problem with the figures?' he said, snapping her out of it.

'Oh.' She put the papers on the desk in front of him. 'Here.'

He picked them up and flipped through them. 'What am I supposed to be seeing?'

She went around the desk to stand next to him, even more aware of his dark attractive aura. She pointed at the numbers. 'Here. I'm sorry, Tony, I have no idea where that two hundred and forty thousand went.'

'Wait.' Tony slid the keyboard from the side of the desk, and pulled up the exchange figures. 'Thought so. That's two hundred thousand Chinese yuan, in Hong Kong dollars.' He smiled up at her. 'Didn't you realise that?'

'Well, yes,' she said. 'But all the transfers to the mainland part of the company are accounted for.' She sagged with defeat. 'I have no idea where that money went. I am so sorry.'

'Don't panic. I gave it to my mother in China,' Tony said. 'Stop tying yourself up in knots about it. Put it down as a charitable donation to an old people's home in Guangzhou.'

'Do you have the receipt?'

He shrugged and pushed the keyboard aside. 'It was cash.'

'But without a receipt – '

'Mei.' He took her hand, and her heart leapt. 'Dear Mei, always looking after me.' Still holding her hand, he stood to face her. He leaned on the desk and gazed into her eyes. 'You are so very perfect. You're beautiful, and clever, and work so hard for me.'

She was speechless, holding his hand and wanting more. His lush, sensitive mouth filled her vision …

He released her hand. 'Don't worry about getting into trouble. Just put it down as a charitable donation – I have the receipt in the Guangzhou office, I'll bring it next time I come.' He handed the papers to her. 'You don't need to ask for permission to come into my office, Mei, you are welcome any time.' He lowered his voice. 'I really like having you close by.'

She went around his desk in a warm daze and opened the door to go out.

'Oh,' he said when she was about to close the door. 'Finish up those accounts, and leave early. I'm sure your family need you. You work too hard, dear Mei, and I know how diligent you are.'

She felt her face reddening as she softly closed the door behind her. He was so *kind*.

She didn't leave work early as Tony had suggested; her role was important to her. She enjoyed the challenge of greater responsibility; since she'd been promoted to senior accountant she'd streamlined many of the antiquated procedures that Nasty Kwok had ignored as too hard to change. Nasty was on the verge of retirement, and if she had his role – if Tony was willing to promote a woman to the position of Chief Finance Officer instead of one of the men – there were so many more improvements she could make. She'd been working on a comprehensive list of all the things that could improve the company, and if she had Nasty's job she could improve both profitability and the working conditions for the staff.

It was dusk when she stepped off the bus at the high-rise estate where the family lived in a three-bedroom apartment. The view from the windows wasn't anything special, looking out over the other high-rises in the estate, but it was high on the thirty-third floor, above the traffic noise from below, and not far from the centre of the city where Mei and her parents worked.

Mei could afford to move out, but even on her salary as a senior accountant she would have to move to something less than two hundred square feet, a long way from her work place. It might change if she ever had a boyfriend and needed more privacy, but right now she had her own room, and sharing the expenses with her parents and brother made life much easier. The whole boyfriend thing was another issue. How would she explain about her mother and little brother to any man? If she started to date Tony – well, in her dreams – how would she explain to him the source of her red hair?

She was the first home, the only member of the family that didn't have people – and animals – relying on them. She went into the kitchen with the vegetables and meat she'd bought at the wet market on the way. She had a fresh fish to steam, leafy vegetables, some chicken for her mother and brother... she hummed to herself as she filled the rice cooker and turned it on.

The front door opened and closed.

'Who is it?' she called from the kitchen.

'Just us,' Ba Ba said. He appeared in the kitchen doorway. 'We stopped to buy some vegies, but Mr Chan at the wet market said you already bought some...' he peered into the sink. 'Wah, nice fish.'

'Di Di brought you home?' Mei said.

'Yeah, he's in the car park.' Ba Ba bustled out of the kitchen. 'Don't cook that fish, I'll do it myself. I want it done right!'

Ma Ma came in, and pecked her on the cheek. 'Ew. Fish. Oh, you bought meat too.' She squeezed Mei around the waist. 'Best daughter.'

Mei smiled and continued to wash the vegetables.

The door opened and Di Di came in. He went straight past the kitchen without saying anything and directly into his bedroom. He charged into the bathroom and turned the water on in the shower shortly after.

'Something happened to him at work today,' Ma Ma said. 'He wouldn't talk about it in the car. Maybe you can wring it out of him.'

'I'll see what I can do.'

Di Di was quiet at dinner, and sat staring at his rice bowl without eating.

Mei picked up a piece of meat in her chopsticks and put it on top of his rice. 'Tell us what happened, Di Di.'

'We all lose patients sometimes,' Ma Ma said. 'We can't save everyone.'

Di Di picked up his chopsticks, and it was like a dam broke. His brown eyes were full of anguish under his bright red hair. 'I delivered a litter of pups today.'

Mei perked up. 'Oh how cute!'

Di Di sagged even further over his bowl. 'Lost every single one of them.'

'They all died?' Ma Ma said. 'Why? Were they premature?'

Di Di dug into the rice with his chopsticks without eating. 'Bulldogs.' His voice trembled with suppressed anger. 'Humans!'

'Hey, Ba Ba and I are human,' Mei said.

Di Di winced. 'Sorry. But it's so depressing. They've inbred these poor dogs to the point that they can't bear live young, they can only have them by caesarean. Hell, they can't even *mate* properly, they need to be inseminated. This was a show-quality purebred bitch, imported from America, and worth a fortune. I inseminated her myself with frozen semen from a grand champion sire last year. *Idiot* human owners brought her in when she'd already been in labour for forty-eight hours. I opened her up to get the pups out, and they were all dead.' He slammed his chopsticks onto the table. 'And then she went septic and I lost her too – my first solo Caesar as an intern and I lose the dog.' He wiped his hand over his eyes. 'It hurts.'

'Will the owners sue the practice?' Ma Ma said.

'No, they signed an indemnity, all bulldog owners have to,' Di Di said. 'That makes them even more upset. They have nobody to blame, nobody to punish.' He shrugged. 'The senior

12

vets were supportive, said that I did nothing wrong, it was a textbook Caesar, and it was the stupid owners that caused the death of the dogs. I think that's the worst part – that nobody blames me. I blame myself.'

'Telling you that it's not your fault right now would be a waste of time, right?' Ba Ba said.

Di Di nodded, studying his rice bowl.

Ba Ba leaned back. 'Put your food in the fridge and go for a run with your mother.'

Di Di's head shot up and his face went blank. He looked from their mother to their father.

'Get the car keys, let's go,' Ma Ma said. She rose. 'Keep the food for us, Mei?'

'I will, Ma Ma,' Mei said.

Ma Ma walked around the dining table and patted Di Di on the shoulder. 'Your father's right. Let's go to Tai Po and chase the monkeys in the moonlight.' She kissed Ba Ba on the top of his bald head. 'I love you.'

He took her hand and squeezed it. 'Be careful.'

'We will.'

Di Di rose from the table, kissed Ba Ba on the top of the head as well, gathered the car keys, and both of them went out.

Mei put her chopsticks down, suddenly not hungry. 'I'll worry about them.'

'So will I, but they need to do this. I was about to suggest it anyway, since the moon is full.' He stood and collected the bowls. 'Let's watch TV while we wait for them to come back.'

She hugged him around the waist, took the rest of the plates, and followed him into the kitchen.

It was two a.m. when Ma Ma and Di Di returned, relaxed and happy with their red hair full of twigs and leaves. Mei jerked awake where she had fallen asleep on her father's shoulder in front of the television, and he snorted awake as well.

'You didn't need to wait up for us,' Di Di said.

'There are traps, and baits, and idiots with pellet guns who would not hesitate to take pot-shots at wild foxes out there,' Ba Ba said. 'And Celestials who will kill fox spirits on sight.'

'Fox spirits who are way too clever for any of that,' Ma Ma said, taking him by the hand and leading him towards their bedroom.

'It was wonderful,' Di Di said to Mei, combing the twigs out of his red hair with his fingers. 'I wish you and Ba Ba could change and join us.'

'I'm happy being what I am, a stupid human,' Mei said with amusement.

Di Di laughed, kissed the top of Mei's own red hair, and headed down towards his own room.

Mei sighed with bliss and turned the television off. She'd be wrecked at work the next day from lack of sleep, but it was worth it to see her mother and brother so happy.

The next morning Mei yawned as she opened the accounting software.

Sandy poked her head over the top of the cubicle divider. 'Mr Wong was here, Mei.'

Mei jolted, thinking she must be late if he'd been around already. She checked the clock; she was right on time, so she raised her eyebrows at Sandy.

'He said he wants to see you at twelve.'

'What for?' Mei said, searching her memory for any reasons the boss could have for speaking to her, and finding none. The two hundred forty was accounted for, and the monthly figures had balanced nicely.

'No idea,' Sandy said, and disappeared behind the divider. Her face reappeared. 'Did you see him in *Happenings*?'

'No?'

Sandy's hand snaked over the divider, holding a copy of the magazine. 'Right up the front. He's famous!'

Mei took the magazine and flipped it open to the first article. There was Tony, attending a movie premiere, in one of the large glossy photos of celebrities on the page. The caption underneath speculated as to why he'd attended alone when he could have any woman in the Territory on his arm.

Mei sighed. He looked even more delicious in the tuxedo, smiling for the cameras, his movie-star good looks glowing in the light of the flash. She studied the picture, imagining herself next to him, rubbing shoulders with billionaires and movie stars and sharing a smile with that delectable piece of gorgeous.

'Look at you all starry-eyed,' Sandy said with amusement. 'You should tell him that you like him, Mei.'

14

'No,' Mei said, handing the magazine back. 'He's big and famous, and I'm just an accountant.'

'You're the smartest one in the office,' Sandy said as she took the magazine. She lowered her voice. 'I hope he gives you Nasty's job when Nasty retires. You'd be great. Look at all the changes you've made already; if you had Nasty's job you wouldn't have him stopping you from getting things done.'

'What about you?' Mei said. 'You'd be good in it as well.'

'I have a husband and two kids to worry about,' Sandy said. 'I don't need that sort of responsibility. No long hours for me! But you'd thrive on it.'

'We'll see what happens when the time comes,' Mei said absently as she opened her email.

'Just make sure you tell me all the details when you come back from your twelve o'clock meeting with him,' Sandy said. She disappeared behind the divider, and her voice was muffled. 'Maybe the meeting is to give you Nasty's job?'

'We'll see what happens,' Mei repeated, and went back to the top of the email list. She'd read three emails and hadn't digested a word of them.

At exactly twelve o'clock, Mei went out to the reception area to find Tony waiting for her, leaning on the reception desk.

'Mr Wong,' she said, 'you wanted to see me?'

'Don't you want to bring your bag? Your phone?' he said.

'My bag?' she said, confused.

'For lunch,' he said.

Her mouth fell open. 'Oh.' She spun to head back to the admin side. 'I'll be right back!'

She quickly grabbed her bag at her desk. 'Why didn't you tell me we were all going to lunch?' she asked Sandy.

'We're not,' Sandy said. She looked around; the other workers were still at their desks. Sandy's eyes widened. 'He's taking you out for lunch?'

Mei's heart leapt. 'Uh... looks like it.'

Sandy grinned and turned back to her screen. 'About time.' She lowered her voice. 'Now I *really* want all the details.'

Tony took Mei to a five-star hotel nearby. She walked beside him up the marble stairs with a balustrade of twining cast-iron in the shape of ivy and roses, admiring its beauty. At the top of the stairs Tony walked straight into the restaurant without stopping at the greeting lectern. The maître d' saw him and escorted them to a table for two at one side of the restaurant, next to the grand piano on its pedestal and under one of the large crystal chandeliers. The two-storey-high room had panels on the walls that were painted with renaissance-style murals of men and women wearing old-fashioned clothing in idyllic pastoral settings.

A waiter swept up, poured water into balloon glasses from a silver carafe, then took the napkins from the table, flicked them open with a flourish, and laid them into Tony and Mei's laps. Tony picked up the menu and seemed to be oblivious to the waiter's attention, and Mei thanked the waiter quietly. The waiter smiled knowingly at her.

Tony ordered wine off the menu in French, and the waiter nodded and swept away.

Tony picked up the food menu. 'This place isn't the best but it's close by and I need to be back at the office by two, so I suppose it will have to do.'

'It's lovely,' Mei said. 'The paintings are beautiful.'

'Pfft.' Tony waved her down. 'They're bad imitations. Art in the Louvre is much better, eh?'

'I've never been,' Mei said, picking up her own menu. She stared at it with bewilderment; none of the Western food meant anything to her. She'd been to Western-style café's with her work mates, but this list of high-end dishes, some of them in French rather than English and without Chinese translations, was incomprehensible.

'Well that's just not good enough,' Tony said. 'Everybody should have the chance to see the Mona Lisa at least once in their lives.' His eyes sparkled at her over the top of his menu. 'Maybe a weekend away in the future. Or a week.' He glanced down at the menu. 'Do you know what you want? I usually get the foie gras to start, then the beef medallion with bone marrow, those are the best things they do here.'

Mei had no idea what foie gras was, but the rest sounded okay – and reassuringly carnivorous: thankfully Tony wasn't vegetarian – so she nodded. 'Sounds good for me too.'

He smiled. 'Excellent choice.'

She put her menu down and took a sip of the water, studying him. He seemed relaxed and comfortable. The waiter arrived with the wine and performed a small ritual of showing Tony the label and letting Tony taste it, then poured it for them, took the order from Tony, and left.

Mei tried the wine; it was red, strong, and not what she was accustomed to – but probably very expensive. 'So why did you want to bring me for lunch, Mr Wong?'

'Tony, please, Mei,' he said. He swirled the wine in his glass and sipped it with relish. 'Love this vintage.' He studied her. 'There's much more to you than meets the eye, dear Mei –'

Her eyes widened. Did he know?

'... And I would love to know more about you. How long has your family lived in Hong Kong? What do your parents do? I've wanted to know more about you for a long time, and after you were so sweet yesterday, I finally felt courageous enough to ask you to come out with me.'

'Oh.'

'So?'

She leaned forward and grinned at him. 'I'll tell you about my family, but you have to tell me about yours.'

'Sure,' he said. 'I'm from Chiu Chow province, in my own dialect we call ourselves Teochew people. My mother came from Swatow, up the Eastern coast of China; she came to Hong Kong escaping the Great Leap Forward. It was either that or starve to death back in the home village.'

'And your father?'

'She left him,' Tony said. He scowled at his wine. 'He was... is... well, let's just say we're better off without him. My mother returned to Swatow, she has a little house outside the city, and I visit her when I go do business in China.' He shrugged. 'You know all about my financial situation and the details of the company, you have the advantage over me there.'

'Brothers and sisters?'

'I have a brother and a sister. They have their own businesses, nothing to do with RedGold.'

'Do they have kids?'

His face went blank. 'I honestly don't know. They're back in China as well, I haven't talked to them in a long time.' He smiled. 'They probably do, they're married.' He sipped his wine. 'Your turn.'

'My mother's a doctor, my father's a nurse, they have a general practice together.'

'They met in a hospital when they were training, did they?'

'Yes they did,' Mei said, impressed by his keen insight. 'And my little brother's training to be a vet, he's doing an internship out in the New Territories.'

'A vet, eh?' he said meaningfully. 'So your mother treats *humans*, and your brother treats *animals*?'

She hesitated at his tone, and studied him, wondering if he knew more than he was expressing. His face gave nothing away, and she decided that he was unaware.

She grinned. 'That's right. Although my mother says that the humans are less reliable than animals, sometimes.'

'There are times when I feel that way myself,' he said. 'Some of my business associates are quite demonic.'

She knew what he was talking about. 'That Mr Chan from the steel company – you know the one?'

He laughed. 'I know! He's such an *ass*. Do you believe that he actually propositioned poor Minty the first time he came to visit me? My own secretary! I wanted to punch him in the nose – Minty has a photo of her two-year-old daughter sitting right there on her desk, and this … man … is saying all these disgusting things to her. I dragged him into my office and gave him a piece of my mind.'

She laughed with him. 'I'm glad you looked after Minty, she's a lovely woman.'

He sobered. 'Not as lovely as you, Mei.'

She opened and closed her mouth, feeling the blush rise on her cheeks. The entrée arrived to rescue her. Tony showed her how to eat the grey paste with the bread, and it was smooth and delicious. The wine buzzed in her head and she relaxed, enjoying Tony's conversation.

It was nearly two o'clock when they finished, and Mei opened her bag and pulled out her wallet to pay for her own food.

'No need,' Tony said, waving to the waiter and holding up a platinum credit card. 'Business expense, covered by the company.'

18

'Are you sure?' she said.

'Of course.'

The waiter brought the check and Tony ran his finger quickly over the figures, then put the credit card into the folder and signed the bill. The waiter took the bill away, and Tony reached into his jacket pocket.

'Oh, I nearly forgot. You should have this, I have no-one else to give it to.'

He handed her a solid gold bracelet – twenty-four carat gold – in a decorative chain. The clasp wasn't spring-loaded, it was a simple S-shape holding the end. Solid gold was too soft to have a clasp; a bracelet like this was designed to be kept on all the time; the pure gold never tarnished and never faded.

She turned the bracelet over in her hands, feeling the weight of the gold. 'I can't take this.'

He gestured towards her. 'Yes you can. It was a gift from one of our suppliers in the Mainland, you might as well have it. Let me put it on you.' He reached towards her and she passed him the bracelet. He took her hand and secured the chain around her wrist, then grinned at her. 'It's just a small token. If it was your wedding gold jewellery, dear Mei, you would be bent with the weight of it. You are worth it.'

She admired the bracelet as it sparkled in the light of the chandelier. The waiter returned with the bill and Tony took it out of the folder.

'Back to work, can't stay around here all day,' he said, rising and putting his arm around her waist to guide her out.

She noticed a few people watching them with interest and felt a small flush of pride to be out with him.

'Although,' he said as her released her to move to a more publicly acceptable distance, 'spending the afternoon here with you sounds like a good idea.'

She linked her arm in his. 'I agree. I hope we can do this again soon.'

He smiled down at her. 'Me too.'

She was still a little light-headed when they returned to the office. She fell into her chair, and Sandy poked her head over the divider.

'Tell all!'

'He's so charming,' Mei said, spinning her chair.

'What did you talk about?'

'Families. Art. Food. I didn't know what foie gras is, and he explained it. It's like shark fin, delicious but so wrong.' She was about to show Sandy the bracelet when she saw her phone on the desk; the light was blinking and she picked it up. 'I forgot my phone and didn't even think of it, I was having so much fun!'

'This is the start of the greatest thing *ever*,' Sandy said with satisfaction. 'He likes you!' She rubbed her hands together. 'Love story of the year. The tycoon and the accountant!'

Mei opened her phone; she had five messages. She scrolled through them and felt a jolt of horror.

MaMa (47 min): DiDi's had an accident meet us at QE2 Hospital

BaBa (34 min): We're at QE2 A&E hurry DiDi's been hurt

MaMa (17 min): The doctors are looking at DiDi and they can't find anything wrong with him either

MaMa (16 min): We're taking him in for tests

BaBa (4 min): Mei where are you? MaMa and the emergency doctors took Leung away for tests and I'm sitting here alone in the A&E waiting room. Are you all right? Please come, I don't know what to do!

She fumbled with the phone and called her father.

'Wei?' he said.

'Ba Ba it's me,' she said. 'I left my phone in the office when I went out for lunch. What happened?'

'Oh, Mei, thank god you called. Leung was attacked. He's unconscious. They found him in an alley behind the vet surgery. The doctors are looking at him…'

'I'm on my way,' Mei said. 'I'll be there as soon as I can.'

Ba Ba's voice cracked. 'Hurry, Mei Mei.'

'Sandy.' Mei jumped up and staggered, still slightly dizzy from the wine. She spoke to Sandy over the divider. 'My brother's hurt. He's in hospital. I have to go.'

'Go,' Sandy said. 'I'll cover for you.'

Mei grabbed her bag and ran.

2

She charged into the waiting room and cast around, looking for Ba Ba. The hospital waiting room had a worn linoleum floor, and tired-looking people in various degrees of shock sat in the rows of chairs. Ba Ba was sitting in the corner, hunched and miserable, his face blank with shock.

She sat next to him and took his hand. 'What happened?'

'They found him in the alley behind the vet's an hour ago. There seems to be some sort of brain damage, but they can't find anything wrong with him.'

'That bulldog,' Mei said, her eyes wide. 'They took revenge on him.'

Ba Ba nodded, and wiped the tears from his cheeks. 'If Di Di comes around and tells us what happened, we'll know for sure. But...' His voice broke, and he put his arm around her to lean into her shoulder. 'He's in a coma, Mei. They can't wake him up.'

'He's special,' she whispered into her father's ear. 'He's stronger than an ordinary human. He's a fox. He's *magical*.'

Ba Ba nodded.

'He'll be all right, just wait and see.' Mei pulled back to smile at him. 'Everything will be fine.'

Ba Ba stiffened in her grasp and Mei turned to see what had affected him. Ma Ma was approaching them, her expression grim.

Mei continued to hold Ba Ba around the shoulders as she spoke to her mother. 'What's the prognosis?'

Ma Ma flopped into the chair next to Ba Ba. 'This is really bad.' She dropped her head into her hands, then straightened and wiped her eyes. 'Really bad.' She lowered her voice so that those around couldn't hear. 'There's nothing physically wrong with him. We can't find an injury; the X-rays are clear. But his mind has been reduced to a baby's.' She spoke even more softly. 'He's been cursed.'

'A curse? Like a *magic* curse?' Mei said with disbelief.

Ma Ma nodded. 'It's a powerful one, too. I've never seen anything like it. We need to find out who owned those bulldogs, because only a demon could do something like this.'

Mei gasped and her hand fluttered to her mouth. 'No.'

'I need to go back inside and talk to them about Di Di. They'll probably want to keep him for a while for observation, but since it's a curse they won't be able to do anything. Go back to work, Mei, I'll see you at home later. Di Di won't die.'

'Can we restore him?' Mei said.

Ma Ma nodded grimly. 'I need to go to Canal Road in Causeway Bay and have a little chat to the women under the overpass there.'

It was nearly four p.m. when Mei returned to the office, dazed and stricken. She hadn't cried; she was still too shocked. She went to her desk, oblivious to everybody around her, and fell into her chair, then opened the accounting software. The numbers blurred on the screen.

'What happened, Mei? You look awful,' Sandy said.

'My brother's in a coma in hospital,' she said absently, staring at the incomprehensible figures.

She didn't really hear the door slam on the other side of the office and only looked up when someone slapped the divider next to her. It was Nasty Kwok.

'And where have you been?' he said, leaning on the divider with menace.

There was a clatter on the other side of the divider, then she hard Sandy's voice mutter.

'My brother...' Mei didn't bother describing the traumatic circumstances, Nasty wouldn't care about her brother, the best she could do was salvage the situation. She stood and bowed to him with her hands clasped in front of her. 'I'm sorry I'm late back, sir, it won't happen again.'

Sandy's mumbles behind the divider became urgent, then she went quiet.

'It had better not,' he said with an ugly light in his eyes. 'Spent too much time shopping, did we?' He eyed her. 'At the salon having your hair dyed that stupid unnatural red colour?'

'I had a family emergency,' Mei said, head bowed in supplication.

'What a pathetic excuse,' he said. 'If you'd told me the truth I'd only you dock you the hours you were away. Since you lied to me, you'll lose your pay for *the whole day*.'

'You will not dock her pay,' Tony said from behind Mei.

Mei jumped and turned. Tony was standing at the divider between her desk and Sandy's, and Sandy was standing with him, small and round next to his slim elegance. Her face was full of triumph.

Tony patted Sandy on the shoulder. 'Thanks, Sandy.'

'My pleasure, sir,' Sandy said smugly, and disappeared behind the divider.

'Did you say you had a family emergency?' Tony said.

'She's lying!' Kwok said.

'My brother...' Mei gathered herself. 'My brother's in the hospital...' It hit her all at once and she couldn't breathe. Her eyes filled with tears and her throat thickened. 'He's in the hospital...' To her horror loud sobs shook her and she couldn't say more. She turned to her desk and yanked some tissues out of the box to wipe her eyes, but her nose was clogged and she couldn't breathe.

Tony bundled her into his arms and held her. She tried to avoid wetting his expensive suit, turning her head away from him. He held her and she clutched him, desperate for the comfort.

'It's okay, it's okay,' he said. 'Let it out.' He raised his voice. 'You are a pathetic excuse for a human being sometimes, Kwok. Go back to your girly movies in your office.'

Kwok sputtered, and Tony interrupted him, his voice echoing through his chest as he held Mei.

'Don't think I don't know what you're up to in there. If it wasn't for Mei our accounts would never balance and I'd probably have the Independent Commission Against Corruption down here asking where all the money I donate to charities goes. Walk softly, my friend, because you really don't want to be fired before you retire, you'll lose your pension.' He rubbed Mei's back. 'Can you walk?'

Mei nodded into his chest.

He moved away and held her around the waist. 'Come with me, I'll get you a drink of water.' He led her through the office and to Mei's complete mortification everybody saw them. She kept the tissues jammed against her face and still occasionally jerked with gasping sobs.

He led her into his office and sat her in one of the visitor's chairs, then took a box of tissues from his own desk and passed it to her.

'You don't need to say anything,' he said. 'Let it out. I'll be right back.'

He left the room and she tried to stop crying while he was gone. She managed to blow her nose and wipe her eyes, the sobs subsiding.

He returned with a glass of water and placed it on his desk, then sat in the other visitor's chair. She took a grateful drink of the water, the sobs still rocking her.

'You are so beautiful,' he said, and that started her off again.

He sat quietly and held her hand while she worked it through. She took a few gasping breaths and nodded to him. 'Thank you.'

'Can you tell me what happened?'

'While we were at lunch, my brother was attacked. He's in a coma in hospital.'

'And you came back to work?' he said incredulously.

She nodded and wiped her eyes again.

'What will I do with you?' he said, with mild exasperation. 'Go home. Look after your family. Come back when you feel better.'

She looked up into his warm brown eyes. 'Are you sure?'

'Of course I'm sure.' He raised her hand to help her stand, then released it. 'Just a minute.' He went around the desk and picked up the telephone. 'Minty? Ask Barnard to bring my car around, to take Miss Lee home. No, she's fine, she just had a family emergency.' He smiled. 'I'll tell her.'

He put the phone down. 'Come and wait outside with me, my driver will take you home. Oh, Minty says that all the people in the office hope your brother is better soon. Sandy heard what you said.'

Mei nodded, clutching the wadded damp tissues. 'Thank you, Tony.'

'Only the best for my dear Mei,' he said with heartbreaking kindness, and took her hand to lead her out to the front of the building. He didn't release her hand until she entered the car, and she didn't want him to.

Mei recognised her mother, standing under the building waiting for a taxi when they arrived. No other woman was as small and slender as Ma Ma, with such bright red hair. Mei quickly thanked Tony's driver, then stepped out of the car to talk to Ma Ma.

'Go up and look after your father,' Ma Ma said.

'Where are you going?' Mei said.

Ma Ma didn't reply.

'If you're going to Canal Road, I want to come too,' Mei said. 'I need to learn about these things from your world. I need to protect myself.'

'You're human, it shouldn't be a problem for you, little Mei,' Ma Ma said. She saw a taxi and waved for it, and it stopped in front of them.

'Di Di was in his human form when it happened to him,' Mei said, following Ma Ma into the cab. 'I'm more than human, I'm half fox too. Besides, I want to hear what they have to say.'

Ma Ma turned to argue with Mei, then gave up and spoke to the driver. 'Causeway Bay, Canal Road.'

Mei settled herself on the seat and closed the door behind her.

The hot, humid air was thick with exhaust fumes when they stepped out of the cab into the concreted undercover area below the Canal Road Overpass. This was the only location in the Territory where elderly women ran small businesses cursing people for cash, and there were four of them with folding tables holding altars and stools in front of them. They all appeared to be more than seventy, wearing traditional black three-quarter pants and brown floral blouses with mandarin collars. The women beat paper cut-outs of the White Tiger God with an old shoe, asking the Tiger to curse whoever their customer selected. Two women were sitting on their stools next to their altars loudly gossiping, while the other two were chanting curses and banging the tiger effigies for sweating customers.

Ma Ma approached the two gossipers and they eyed her warily.

'Have either of you placed a curse on Lee Leung recently?' Ma Ma asked. 'If you have, and you can lift it, I'll pay double.'

25

'Lee Leung?' the first woman said. 'Is Lee the family name?'

Ma Ma nodded. 'Family name, yes.'

The woman pulled out a Hello Kitty notepad and flipped it open. 'No Lee Leung. Roseflower?'

The other woman checked a notepad. 'No Lee Leung.' She gestured towards the other two women, who were still busy chanting curses for their rapt customers. 'They'll be finished soon.'

Mei studied the curse accoutrements with interest. She couldn't see how something so mundane as a cut-out paper tiger and an old shoe could do so much damage.

They waited in the choking air for the other women to stop cursing people. Once the women had bashed the paper tigers for about ten minutes, they burnt them at the altar and assured the customers that the object of their wrath would have terrible luck.

'I can't understand why anyone would do this,' Mei said softly, watching the satisfied customers walk away.

Ma Ma went up to the other two women. 'Have you cursed Lee Leung? If you can remove the curse I'll pay double.'

One woman picked up a notebook. 'No Lee Leung.'

'Me neither,' the other woman said. 'Maybe a freelance witch?'

'Do you know of any?' Ma Ma said. 'I thought you four were the only ones.'

'Only us!' one of the first pair shouted.

Ma Ma hissed under her breath. 'Mei we need to go now.'

'Oh, the Tiger's here,' one of the women said. 'You can ask him, he knows everything.'

'The Tiger's here?' Mei said. She looked up and saw a burly man with a shock of white hair, a ruggedly handsome golden face, and light tawny eyes, approaching them. He wore a tan-coloured suit that complemented his golden skin and white hair. He saw them and his face went hard; his demeanour changed from good-looking gentleman to fierce warrior. He held his hand out and a sword appeared in it, and Mei went cold all the way to her feet.

'Mei run!' Ma Ma said. She grabbed Mei by the arm and dragged her across the road against the lights, making the cars stop and sound their horns. Ma Ma looked back. 'We need to disappear.' She ran for a few hundred metres, then ducked into the lobby of the next building and bolted into the stairwell dragging Mei with her. She charged up the stairs and Mei followed her.

Ma Ma stopped after what seemed like a million floors and cocked her head, then sniffed the air.

'Is he following us?' Mei said.

'No. I don't think so,' Ma Ma said. 'He may have decided I'm not worth the bother. I can't smell him.' They both went quiet and listened. No footsteps came up the stairs.

Ma Ma collapsed against the stairwell wall and wiped her forehead. 'That bastard's been trying to murder me for a long time.'

'But he's a Celestial,' Mei said. 'They have rules. They're supposed to be the *good guys*.'

'When it comes to foxes they don't care,' Ma ma said. 'They'll destroy us if they see us.'

'Wait here,' Mei said. 'I'll go back down quietly and see if he's still around.'

Ma Ma nodded her appreciation.

Mei pulled her suit jacket off; the heat was stifling in the stairwell that reeked of urine and diesel. She eased quietly down the stairs, taking much longer to go down than they had going up. She poked her nose out of the stairwell on the ground floor, and saw the usual afternoon workers leaving the building. She went out of the building and looked up and down the street. No Tiger.

She put her head back inside the stair well and spoke softly. 'All clear, Ma Ma.' She waited for her mother to come down the stairs and they returned home in a taxi, morose.

3

Twelve months later Mei dragged herself into the office, yawning. This was the fifth sleepless night in a row where the entire family had been kept awake by Di Di's uncontrollable convulsions.

'Bad night?' Sandy said over the divider.

Mei nodded. 'He kept us up all night. He screams.' She ran her hand over her bun and tucked a stray lock of hair into it. 'He seems to be getting worse, he spends more and more nights awake.'

'That's awful. Your poor family.'

Mei nodded. 'Ma Ma's had to take the day off again, she took over from my father in the middle of the night, he fell asleep and Leung nearly jumped out the window.' She wiped her eyes. 'Ma Ma's losing patients because she keeps cancelling the appointments. She may have to close the clinic.'

'What about that nurse you hired to look after him?'

'He attacked her last week, and was halfway out the window before Ba Ba managed to pull him down. It has to be one of my parents, he attacks anyone except family members – and with him awake all night it's turning into a full-time job for both of them.'

Sandy lowered her voice. 'Have you thought about putting him in a home?'

'We tried that too,' Mei said. 'He'd keep attacking everybody, and they'd throw him out. We've asked every place in the Territory that could take him, and a couple on the Mainland as well. Nobody will have him.'

'Will the Government help? Surely a charity or something…'

Mei snorted with grim laughter. 'Sandy, this is Hong Kong. Low taxes are good but that means no social welfare for anyone. Look at the old women collecting cardboard for fifty cents a day.'

'Tony's back from China next week. You should ask him for some help. I'm sure he wouldn't mind.'

Mei hesitated, then nodded. 'I know my parents wouldn't like it, but I think we're at the point where if we don't ask for help we'll lose our apartment.'

Sandy tapped the top of the divider as she turned away. 'Good to hear.' She turned back and grinned at Mei. 'Have you missed him while he's away?'

Mei's heart tugged in her chest. 'A little.'

'Oh come on, you've been moping around miserable the whole time. You light up when he's around.'

Mei could feel herself blushing. 'Maybe.' She grinned at Sandy. 'Maybe I just miss my fancy five-star lunches with the boss, talking about art, theatre and music.'

'You two are so perfect together,' Sandy said. 'Whoops, Nasty's on the warpath. Heads down.' She disappeared behind the divider.

Mei concentrated on her computer as Nasty stormed past. He stopped and glared at her, and she returned his gaze, innocent. He turned the stare on Sandy, who wasn't visible on the other side of the divider.

He snorted loudly with contempt. 'Gossiping women,' he said, and continued through the office.

'Asshole,' Sandy whispered, loud enough for Mei to hear.

Mei giggled as she sorted through the mail in her inbox. Mostly invoices to deal with, a few bank statements, but one blank envelope addressed directly to her as well – and it didn't look like someone trying to sell her a credit card.

She slitted it open. It was a single piece of paper with a two-line, unsigned message.

I can fix your brother. I know what is wrong with him. Meet me in the Mayfair Hotel lobby at 1pm.

She looked at her clock. Ten am. This would be the longest three hours in history.

She arrived at the Mayfair fifteen minutes early and stood in the lobby, watching all the people go in and out. None of them looked like the sort of person who could help her.

'Lee Mei?' someone said behind her, and she turned. It was a schoolgirl, in a white uniform with badges from one of the local high schools.

'You?' Mei said.

'Come and sit, let's talk,' the girl said, leading Mei to the lobby lounge. Barrel chairs and leather couches were spread across the double-storey area with floor-to-ceiling glass that overlooked Hong Kong harbour. A waiter came up and the student ordered iced lemon tea.

Mei ordered the same thing as she studied the girl. She had long black hair in twin ponytails, was covered in pimples, and appeared to be about fifteen. She didn't look anything like someone who could help Mei, and Mei wondered if she'd just been duped into buying an ordinary schoolgirl an expensive drink. The girl's friends were probably somewhere nearby laughing at her. But the note …

'Let's get straight to business,' the girl said, and her tone was all adult.

'What's your name?' Mei said.

'Irrelevant,' the girl said. 'You can call me… Fua. Whatever.' She brushed it aside. 'I know about your brother. He's been cursed because some puppies died in his care.'

Mei's heart leapt with hope and suspicion. 'How do you know?'

'That's also irrelevant,' Fua said. 'Did you find out who did it? If you know who did it you can have them undo it.'

'The records were erased at the veterinary practice,' Mei said. 'We checked and they're gone. Nobody there has any memory of the dogs' owners. My brother is the only one who knows what they look like. We have no idea how to uncurse him. How come you do?'

'The important thing that I know is how to fix him.'

'How could you…' Mei's breath faded as she realised what she was talking to. 'Are you some sort of demon in a schoolgirl form?'

'Not a demon. I'm a Celestial, so you know you can trust me. I'm exiled from Heaven because of a … romantic entanglement, and I keep this form to hide from the Celestial authorities. But I need to make a living, and that's hard as a child. So I'll take the curse off your brother.'

'Make a living?' Mei said suspiciously. 'How much will you charge us for this?'

'Twenty million dollars.'

Mei made a loud bark of laughter and few heads turned in their direction. 'Don't be ridiculous!'

The teas arrived and Fua looked pointedly at Mei when the waitress put the bill on the table. Mei handed her a credit card, but not before wincing at the hotel prices. Two iced lemon teas came to nearly a hundred dollars that she really couldn't afford. With Ma Ma's practice failing, Mei's salary was supporting all four of them.

Fua jammed the lemon slices into her tea with the long spoon. 'Twenty million. Your mother's a doctor, you can afford it.'

'She's not working at the moment!' Mei said. 'What can we negotiate? Twenty million is insane!'

'That's my offer.' Fua rose and placed a plain white business card on the table. 'Contact me if you find the twenty million.'

'Wait,' Mei said. 'You may be a fraud. How do I know you can uncurse my brother?'

Fua stared down at Mei, and Mei's chest constricted. She tried to breathe and nothing happened. Her heart pounded, and her head felt like it would explode. She desperately tried to gasp for breath and couldn't. Black spots appeared in front of her eyes and a rushing sound filled her ears …

The pressure released and Mei collapsed forward, gasping for breath.

'I'm an accomplished sorceress, and I can fix your brother.' Fua tapped the card. 'Call me when you gain some common sense.'

'It's not common sense I'm lacking, it's cash!' Mei said as Fua strolled away and out of the hotel.

Mei picked up the card. It had a mobile phone number on it and nothing else. Mei slipped the card into her bag and headed back to the office. Perhaps Ma Ma had an idea about the schoolgirl, because Mei certainly didn't have any.

'A schoolgirl?' Ma Ma said over dinner. 'Not unusual. I took that form myself for a while, but it's not worth the trouble with finding an income. Excellent way to hide from the Celestial authorities, though.'

Ba Ba was busy feeding Di Di, who grunted loudly and tried to push the food away. 'Hiding from the authorities?'

'Plenty of people like to avoid Celestial scrutiny, not just foxes.' Ma Ma studied the card, then sniffed it. She frowned. 'Smells of demon.'

'What if that schoolgirl is a demon? Can she still lift the curse?' Mei said.

'She'd be the best person to do it, actually, since a demon did it to him in the first place,' Ma Ma said. 'Demons will occasionally curse people to gain extra income, but they take a big risk if a Celestial catches them doing it. Instant death sentence.'

Mei gasped. 'She's the one cursed Di Di in the first place!'

'That's obvious,' Ma Ma said.

'Did you ever do that, Red?' Ba Ba said without looking away from Di Di.

Ma Ma saddened. 'I'm offended that you even need to ask that. And no, of course not.'

'But you know how demons work?' Ba Ba said, pushing the point.

Ma Ma's tone was still sad. 'I may have had business dealings with them – but it was a long time ago. Every demon I worked with paid their bill on time and kept their word.' She winced. 'It was the *Celestials* who were a problem, the White Tiger...' She took a deep breath and changed direction. 'She can probably do what she says. She can uncurse him.'

'So where do we find twenty million dollars?' Ba Ba said.

'We don't,' Ma Ma said, and tossed the card onto the table. 'Even if we sell the unit, we would only get about six million for it. And the mortgage is nearly that much already.' She ran her hand through her red bob. 'We can't pay the mortgage as it is. The bank want to see me. I'm sorry, Mei.' She gasped. 'Your father and I aren't making enough to cover the repayments. We have to close the clinic. We're going to lose the unit.'

'If I gave you all my salary would it cover the repayments?' Mei said.

'Yes,' Ma Ma said. 'But with nothing left over for luxuries like food.'

'Oh.'

'We will find something,' Ba Ba said. 'As long as we're together.'

Two weeks later Mei yawned as she opened the email program; she'd helped out during the night, as both her parents were constantly exhausted. She skimmed through the messages and saw one from Tony.

To: Mei Lee

From: Tony Wong

Mei I want to see you as soon as you come in

She felt a thrill of delight; he was back. It had been a long three weeks waiting for him to return, and he wanted to see her straight away. She felt the same way; she'd missed him so much and been so lonely without him.

'I have to go see Tony,' she said over the cubicle wall to Sandy.

'He's back?' Sandy said. She shooed Mei away. 'Go. Run!'

Mei walked quickly out to reception, and was buzzed through to the executive side. Tony's secretary smiled at Mei. 'Go right in.'

Mei tapped on Tony's office door, then opened it to peer around, ensuring that she wasn't disturbing him.

'About time!' Tony said. 'Come in, come in.'

She went in and closed the door behind her, then sat in the visitor's chair.

Tony was studying his computer monitor. 'I need your advice. Kwok Kam's due to retire.' He turned away from the monitor to face her. 'Who should I appoint as new CFO?'

Mei opened and closed her mouth a few times, then took a giant leap of faith. 'Me. I can do it.'

'No,' Tony said, turning back to the screen. 'Who else is suitable?'

She screwed up her courage and pushed it. She knew she could do this. 'You won't give me the job of CFO? I think I'm the most qualified,' she said.

'True, but...' He waved one hand at her without looking away from the screen. 'Someone else.'

'See? Even you say I'm the most qualified. I can do it, Tony. Trust me. If you don't think I can, how about you try me out for six months in the role, but in my current salary? Let me prove myself to you.'

He faced her and leaned his arms on the desk. The dimples appeared as he smiled, and she desperately willed herself not to become lost in his eyes.

'It can't be you, Mei,' he said, and waved her down when she opened her mouth to protest again. 'Because I'm promoting you to CEO. I'm spending too much time in the China office, and I need someone to run the Hong Kong side of the company in my absence.'

Mei closed her mouth with a snap.

He continued to smile at her, and raised his index finger. 'One condition, though.'

She tilted her head. 'What?'

'Uh...' He threw himself out of his chair and stalked to the ornaments displayed on the back wall. 'Before I tell you the condition, I have to explain something about myself.' He turned and leaned on the shelves. 'I know this will be hard to believe, but I'm not exactly ... human, Mei.'

Oh lord, he was a Celestial. Ma Ma had said that the Shen – the sprits – of Heaven sometimes had businesses on the Earth, and Tony was one of them. The minute he found out what her mother was – foxes were regarded by many Celestials as demonic avatars of malicious troublemaking – he would refuse to have anything to do with Mei.

She straightened in her seat, waiting for the blow to fall. She would retain her dignity, and leave her job before he had a chance to discover her true nature. She had been unbelievably lucky that he'd never seen her family in the two years she worked there. Ma Ma's natural caution had paid off.

She studied him carefully, probably for the last time. She would never see him again after this, she'd have to go into hiding. She gazed at him, devastated. Her world was falling to pieces around her.

Tony stood next to the bookshelves, deep in thought. He hadn't said anything in a while and she snapped out of her daydream.

'Not human?' she said.

'I'm trying to rise above what I am,' he said. 'Humans have a word for us... ' He grimaced. 'That's not what I am any more. I've changed.' He came back to the desk and took her hand across its surface. His skin was cool and silken. 'You've made me see that there is so much more to life, and that it's important to be kind and caring for others. I'm not a demon any more, I'm trying to be better than that.'

34

'A *demon*?' she squawked, jumping to her feet and yanking her hand away.

'I used to be,' he said. 'But you showed me how to be better.' He took her hand again. 'You're a fox, aren't you? You have that bright red hair... the Celestials hate you as much as they hate us.'

'I'm not a fox,' she said.

'Please don't lie to me,' he said. 'If you're a fox, I can protect you. I can protect your family. Even though I'm trying to be better, I'm still a powerful demon, and under my protection your family would be completely safe from Celestials for the rest of their lives.' He walked around the desk so that he was standing close to her, and squeezed her hand. 'Don't lie to me, Mei, you're better than that. Your honesty and integrity are an inspiration to me.'

She lowered her head; he was right. She shouldn't lie when he'd just told her the truth about himself. 'My mother's a fox. My father's human.'

'That explains your brilliance. Your intelligence. Your spark,' he breathed.

She looked up into his eyes, and he was gazing at her with compassion tempered by ... more than kindness. His expression was full of adoration.

'I'm half-fox. All I inherited from my mother was the hair,' she said, then realised that she'd lied without a second thought. 'No. I'll tell you the whole truth: I inherited a better sense of smell, some healing ability, and natural agility as well.'

'I would like to meet your mother one day. How old are you really?'

She shook her head. 'I haven't lied about anything else. I'm really twenty-seven.' She had a horrible thought. 'If you're a demon ... how old are you?'

He nodded. 'I don't lie either. I'm thirty-five.' He quirked a small smile. 'Just a baby, by demon standards, but old enough to know that life isn't for me. You've shown me that kindness is so much better than cruelty, and I want to give you something in return. Be chief executive for me, on this side of the office. You can do it, you're smart and capable and the only one I trust.'

A bolt of recognition swept through her. 'My brother's been cursed by a demon. Do you think you could free him?'

'Probably, I'd need to see him first, but there's a good chance I can. There's still one condition for all of this, though.'

'What's that?' she said suspiciously.

'Marry me, Mei, you make me a better man and I want to be with you – learn goodness from you, be human with you – for the rest of your life.'

He slipped his arm around her waist, pulled her in, and kissed her. She hesitated with shock for a moment, but it felt so good that she surrendered to the heat of the kiss and slid her hands over the fine, smooth cotton of his business shirt and the chiselled muscles of his back beneath. His hands drifted down over her behind and pulled her into him, and she felt how much he wanted her. Her brain stopped working and it was all sensation as she melted into him.

He broke the kiss and they held each other, breathless. Mei felt the heat on her cheeks. She'd never been with a man, she'd never trusted anyone enough to let them come this close to her. Since she'd started at RedGold two years before, she'd only had eyes for Tony. Her dreams were coming true.

'Marry me,' he whispered with is arms around her. 'You're capable of so much more. Be my wife, my business partner, my everything. I know it's the heat of the moment, but I love you, Mei, and I want to give you everything I have.'

She looked up into his intense face, golden in the midday light through the windows. Her voice wasn't working.

'Is that a yes?' he said.

She closed her eyes for a moment to gather herself, and breathed deep of his scent. The acrid smell was coming from *him*, it was the smell of demon.

'I need time to think about it,' she said.

'Take all the time you need,' he said. 'Kwok is leaving in two weeks. You have plenty of time...' He bent to speak closely to her. 'To say yes.'

'I need to talk to my family,' she said.

'Of course you do. Go,' he said. 'Take the rest of the day off. Ask them what they think. If they want to meet me, let me know.'

'One more thing.'

'This?' he said, and kissed her again.

It was a long time before the broke the kiss, and his hands had found their way inside her blouse. She stepped back and he gently released her.

'Please say yes,' he said. 'To both things. You'd be a fantastic CEO, and as my wife you could have complete control of the company, run everything independently. Provided it continues to make a profit, I wouldn't interfere at all. Please make me happy by marrying me, because I really do love you.'

She nodded without speaking, too confused to reply. She stumbled out of his office and was through the main doors and in the street before she realised that she'd left her bag and wallet at her desk. She returned to retrieve them without speaking to anyone, and went out the door to find a taxi to take her home.

Mei's father was in the cramped living room of their new housing estate flat, sitting next to Di Di in his wheelchair in front of the television. Unpacked boxes sat on one side, making the tiny space even smaller; the entire flat was a rectangle of ten by five metres, with a thin wooden divider down the middle to separate the living and sleeping spaces.

Ba Ba rose when he saw Mei. 'What happened? Why are you here?'

Mei opened and closed her mouth, then said, 'I need to speak to Ma Ma. Urgently. Both of you.'

'She's asleep, it was a bad night.' He gestured towards Di Di, who seemed half-asleep as well. 'It took both of us to stop him from bashing his brains out on the window bars.' He lowered his voice. 'Is something the matter, Mei Mei? Are you all right? It's urgent?'

'It's not a matter of life or death,' Mei said. 'Tony asked me to marry him!'

'What, Tony the boss, the one in the suit?' Ba Ba said.

'Yes! He wants me to marry him and be CEO of the whole Hong Kong operation!'

'And what did you say?'

'I said I needed to think about it.'

'You need to talk to your mother before you give him your answer. What she is – '

The door in the divider opened, and Ma Ma came out wrapping a robe around herself. 'I thought I heard talking. What happened, Mei? You're completely white. Are you all right?'

Mei gestured for Ma Ma to join her on the couch.

'My boss, Tony.' Mei tilted her head slightly. 'We've been going out for a while now, it's been pretty serious...'

Ma Ma waved it away. 'We know that, Mei, it's obvious.'

'He asked me to marry him.'

'And you said you needed to think about it,' Ba Ba said. He shared a look with Ma Ma. 'Sounds like an excellent match to me.'

'He's a demon,' Mei said.

There was complete silence for a long time. Mei's heart thumped in her ears.

'He says he's changed, he wants to be a better person,' she said.

'Can that happen?' Ba Ba said.

'Yes,' Ma Ma said. 'Look at the White Snake: fell in love with a human and became a model wife. So you worked for him for two years and never knew?'

Mei shook her head. 'He's always been kind to me.' She had a small warm feeling of achievement. 'He says I make him a better person, that being around me has changed him.'

Ma Ma nodded. 'It can happen. I've had dealings with Earthly-based demons and they've always been trustworthy business partners who paid their bills and kept their word. Celestials on the other hand...'

'Do you love him?' Ba Ba said abruptly. 'Or are you just star-struck by the chance of being Tai Tai to a tycoon, and being in charge of the whole company?'

'I think I do love him,' Mei said. 'I'm so unhappy when he's not around. But I need to know, from you, if it's possible for a demon to be a good husband to me.'

'If he has changed, it could be extremely beneficial for the family,' Ma Ma mused. 'A powerful demon could protect us from the Celestials. You'd never have to fear that you, me or Di Di would be arrested for being what we are, just because we have red hair.'

'That's what Tony said,' Mei said. 'He knows that foxes are targets, and he said he'd protect us. All of us.'

'And he's aware of the world of Shen, so we don't need to explain anything about ourselves and deal with any sort of judgement,' Ma Ma said.

'He said he may be able to uncurse Di Di, as well,' Mei said.

Ba Ba sat straighter. 'Really?'

'That's possible.' Ma Ma nodded to herself, making a decision. 'Dinner with him, the whole family together. I want to meet this demon and see if he speaks the truth.'

'Yes,' Mei said, relieved. 'You have a gift: you can always tell when someone's speaking the truth.'

4

'The demon paid in full, in silver,' Ma Ma said as they sat around the restaurant's table waiting for Tony. He'd booked a private room for them in an upmarket Cantonese restaurant, with fine table linen and a wide-screen television for karaoke parties. 'Then the Shen turned up and destroyed it. I was lucky to make it out alive. But the demon was the one who –' She stopped when Tony opened the door.

He hesitated in the doorway, and Mei went to him to clasp her arm in his.

She turned to the family: slim, gentle Ma Ma, round jolly Ba Ba, and Di Di sitting boneless and oblivious in his wheelchair. It was important to her that the family accept Tony, she wanted a harmonious relationship between them all. From Tony's face he felt the same way.

'This is Tony Wong.' She gestured towards her family. 'My mother, Hong Lai. My father, Lee Sai Chung, and my brother, Lee Leung.'

Tony extended his hand towards Mei's father over the table, and Mei's father sat looking at it for a long uncomfortable moment. Tony pulled his hand back, and Mei glared at her father. He didn't seem to notice her, his attention was focussed on Tony.

Tony squeezed Mei's arm and sat, guiding her down to sit next to him. 'I'm honoured to meet Mei's family. You must be special to have a daughter as smart and honest as she is.'

Ba Ba didn't relax. Di Di noticed Tony, and made loud garbled noises, waving his hands.

'You've taken the name Wong? Are you a demon prince?' Ma Ma said.

Tony hesitated, then said, 'Yes.'

'Spawn of the King himself?'

'Yes.'

Mei glanced at Tony. She hadn't known that, but then again she didn't know much about demons at all. He was a prince?

'I have no contact with my father,' Tony said. 'My Mother escaped the Nests and took me and my siblings with her. She wants no part of demon politics; she just wants to be left in peace, and I want to be left alone to run my business.' He put his hand on Mei's. 'I live as a human, and Mei has shown me a path that is different from anything I've ever seen.' He squeezed her hand. 'She's taught me that kindness is more important than power. She's inspired me to be a better man.'

'I can understand why you'd want to do that,' Ma Ma said. 'I've been there myself. Is your father pursuing you? Does he try to return your Mother to the Nests?'

Mei glanced at Ma Ma, hearing the capital letters.

'We stay well away from the King,' Tony said. 'My Mother has done her best to make my father think she's dead.'

Mei heard the capital letter again. It made the word "mother" sound ominous.

'Why do you want to marry Mei?' Ma Ma said. 'Your kind don't feel love.'

'Some of us do,' Tony said. 'Mei is the most talented accountant I've ever had. The company has thrived under her direction, I'd be lost without her. That's probably due to the gifts she's inherited from you.'

'It has nothing to do with what my mother is,' Mei said.

'No, Mei, he's right,' Ma Ma said. 'Foxes are renowned for being fast and clever and cunning business dealers. He probably worked it out before he even saw me, because of how smart you are.'

'Actually, I didn't,' Tony said. 'Mei looks completely human to me, despite the bright red hair. I thought she dyed it.' He smiled at Mei. 'I was smitten with her before she told me what you are, Mrs Hong. She's clever and sweet and has a heart of pure gold. Sometimes my kind just want to touch something as good as her in the dark lives we lead.'

'Don't let the darkness touch her.'

Tony nodded. 'Never. You can trust me.'

Ba Ba hadn't spoken, but he had been listening attentively, and he sat back and relaxed. Mei's heart leapt; the family believed Tony and if Ma Ma gave her permission, he would agree to it.

'So what will happen to her if we agree to this and she marries you?' Ma Ma said.

'She will be accepted into my family, and all of us will protect her,' Tony said. 'She will have complete control over the

41

Hong Kong side of the business while I manage my affairs on the mainland. The rest of your family will be protected as well, no Celestial will risk approaching a fox who has such high-level demonic links.'

'And my son?' Ba Ba said.

'I think I can uncurse him,' Tony said. 'It looks like a demonic curse. If I can't do it, I know someone who can.'

Mei squeezed Tony's hand and he smiled at her.

Ma Ma and Ba Ba shared a look. Di Di had settled, and sat silently glowering at Tony.

'How old are you?' Ma Ma said.

'Thirty-five,' Tony said.

'Can you show us your True Form?'

Mei heard the capital letters again.

'As the Dark Lady said to the Jade Emperor, this is my True Form,' Tony said. 'This is me. Now that I've learnt compassion from Mei, I want to be nothing but human for her for the rest of my life.'

Ma Ma leaned over the table to speak intensely to him. 'Do you love Mei?'

Tony took a deep breath. 'Yes I do. With all my heart. I would do anything for her, and I will care for and protect your family because it will make her happy.'

Ma Ma leaned back, her expression still severe. She nodded. 'Very well then.' She turned her attention to Mei. 'I think we should discuss Tony's nature before you make a final decision, Mei. You need to understand what you're getting into.'

'No,' Mei said. 'That doesn't matter. I've known Tony for more than two years, and I love him...' She hesitated as she realised that it was true. She did love him. 'I love him and I want to be with him.' She turned to Tony. 'Yes, I'll marry you, Tony.'

His face lit up with a huge grin of joy. 'I think this is the happiest day of my life,' he said.

'You sure, Red?' Ba Ba said softly.

'No,' Ma Ma said. 'But he's telling the truth.' She glared at Tony. 'Mostly.'

'Mostly?' Mei said.

'He's not thirty-five,' Ma Ma said.

Tony stiffened beside Mei.

Mei jerked her hand away. 'You lied to us about your age?'

'I've ruined everything. I am so sorry, Mei.' Tony clasped his hands on the table and looked down. 'But if I told you the truth – that I'm over a hundred years old – would you still want to marry me?'

Mei hesitated, then said, 'Yes.'

His head jerked up and he looked into her eyes. 'You'd accept me even then?'

Mei didn't hesitate. 'Yes I would.'

'You really are exceptional,' he breathed with wonder.

She smiled. 'That's why you want to marry me.'

'Is that all he lied about?' Ba Ba said.

'Yes,' Ma Ma said. 'The rest is the truth.'

'He really loves our Mei and wants to protect her? And all of us?'

'Yes,' Ma Ma said, obviously relenting. 'He really loves her.'

'Then let's order before the restaurant throws us out, because I'm starving!' Ba Ba said, picking up the menu to flip through it.

Tony slipped his arm around Mei to whisper in her ear. 'I'm sorry I lied to you. I didn't want to risk losing you.'

'You'll never lose me,' she said.

He patted her on the back. She pulled him closer and kissed him on the cheek.

After the waiter had taken their order, Ba Ba asked Tony, 'Have you decided on a lucky date for the wedding yet?'

'No. I suppose we need to find one,' Tony said. 'We'll ask a fung shui master.'

'I can do the fung shui and choose a date for you,' Ma Ma said. 'I have some experience in spiritual matters.'

'Of course,' Tony said. 'I have … senior family members that must be honoured, so we'll need to have a traditional ceremony at my home Nest. After that I'll bring her back here to Hong Kong for the legal wedding you can attend. My family won't harm Mei, her quick wits and intelligence are more than welcome into my clan.'

'I don't want my daughter to see a demon's Nest,' Ma Ma said. 'I know what happens in them.'

Mei jolted with concern. 'What happens in them?'

'Nothing,' Tony said. 'Mei will not see anything that will distress her, I promise.' He smiled at Mei. 'Don't worry, it's a lovely house in the countryside. We live as humans.' He nodded to Ma Ma. 'I will protect her and keep her safe.'

Ma Ma looked from Mei to Tony, unconvinced.

'Trust me, I love her and I'll protect her,' he said.

Ma Ma hesitated.

'I'll be fine,' Mei said.

Ma Ma sighed. 'All right.'

When the meal was over Ba Ba asked for the bill.

'I have my car, I'll take you home,' Tony said. 'I'm part of the family.'

'No need, no need,' Ba Ba said, protesting.

'I insist,' Tony said.

'We can make our own way!' Ba Ba said.

'Ba Ba,' Mei said. 'He is part of the family now, he is your son. And taking a taxi with Di Di is a pain, you know that. Tony's car has plenty of room. Let him.'

'Just this once,' Ba Ba said.

'I'll pay for the meal,' Tony said, and raised his hand when Ba Ba began to protest again. 'I know the situation. Let me help.' He smiled at Mei next to him. 'Just this once.'

Ba Ba sighed with defeat.

Tony pulled his huge black Mercedes into the lay-by next to the entrance to the family's building and they all piled out of the car. Tony watched with amusement as Mei helped her parents to put Di Di into his wheelchair.

When they were sorted, Tony put his hands in his pockets and turned to stare up at the building. It was a slab-style from the early sixties; a ten-floor rectangle with a central corridor and one-room apartments on either side, each with a miniscule balcony and bamboo poles sticking out of the wall, draped with wet laundry.

'Your work record says you live in the nice estate in Diamond Hill,' Tony said. 'What are you doing here in this rubbish hole in Cheung Sha Wan?'

'We lost our apartment in Diamond Hill,' Mei said. 'This is all we can afford on my salary.'

'Not any more, now that you're CEO.' Tony turned to Ba Ba and Ma Ma, jovial. 'It makes me look bad having my in-laws in a place like this. Start looking for something better, okay?'

Ma Ma and Ba Ba went on either side of Di Di's chair to carry him up the steps to the lift lobby.

'Let me,' Tony said, and lifted the wheelchair, grinning Di Di and all, up the stairs by himself.

'Wah,' Ba Ba said, standing back and watching with wonder.

'He hardly weighs anything,' Tony said, and put Di Di gently back on the ground. 'You go up first, I want to talk to Mei.'

Ma Ma and Ba Ba shared a knowing look.

'Don't "talk" for too long,' Ba Ba said with amusement as he wheeled Di Di towards the lifts.

Tony backed down the stairs to Mei. The housing estate buildings were open at the ground floor with half-dead grass around the concreted lift lobby, the walls black with mould and car exhaust. 'My future wife deserves much better than this, and tomorrow as soon as you're settled in your office I want you looking for a new place to live.' He leaned in to speak softly to her. 'Until you move in with me, that is.'

She put her arm around his waist. 'I cannot wait. With you every minute of the day? A dream come true.'

He put his arms around her. 'I want to be with you right now,' he said.

She pulled back to see him. 'I'd rather wait until we're properly married.'

'Close enough, we have your parents' permission, your mother's setting a date...' He brushed his lips over her hair. 'I don't want to wait any more for you.' His voice became soft and breathy. 'I want you so much.'

'I suppose we can,' she said, wanting to please him now that they were engaged. It would be just as special, they didn't need a ceremony. 'But it's a long way to your place and then back here.'

He took her hand and led her to the car. 'This will do. The back seat's huge.'

'Someone will see us through the car windows!'

He waved one hand and the windows went black. She gasped with shock.

He smiled. 'I can do all sorts of things. Special things.' He held her close. 'If the parking inspector comes past they won't even see the car. Nobody will see us.' He smiled down at her. 'We're officially engaged. Let's have a little in-car celebration.'

She stepped back. 'I don't want my first time to be in a car. I want it to be special.'

'Your first time?' he said with shock. 'I'm your first?'

She nodded.

'I want you even more. Don't make me wait any longer.' He pulled her into him and ran his fingers over the bracelet he'd given her. 'I've waited for you long enough, my lovely Mei, if I have to wait another moment it will kill me. There's plenty of room in the car, and the first time won't be good for you anyway. Let me have this now, and when we're at my Mother's house we can take our time, and I'll show you how pleasurable it can be.'

She relaxed into him, and he pulled her tighter. She felt herself giving in, she wanted to please him more than anything. It didn't matter anyway, they would be married. His hand went from her wrist to her waist and he breathed into her hair.

'Please give me this now, to seal our engagement. I love you so much, I don't want to wait another minute.' He put his hand on her cheek. 'You do love me, don't you? You'll do this for me? I need you so much.'

She didn't reply, she just opened the car door, climbed in and turned around on the seat. He came in to sit next to her, and shut the door. He pushed her down so she was lying on her back on the seat and wiggled so that he was on top of her.

'Comfortable?' he said.

'Hmm,' she said into the side of his neck.

'Now comes the fun part,' he said, sliding his hands up under her skirt. 'Undressing in the back of a car should be an Olympic sport.' His fingers pushed inside her panties and stroked her, making her arch her back with pleasure. 'But this first time...' He pulled her panties down to her knees, then leaned sideways to unzip himself. 'I think we'll just do it with the clothes on.'

She felt raw and exposed as she went up the lifts, sure that what she'd just done was stamped on her forehead. There had been blood and pain, and Tony had assured her that it was normal, and that next time would be much more pleasurable. He'd even helped her clean up, gentle and sympathetic.

The metal sheeting around the lower half of the lift wall was rusting away; it had been installed to stop the wood walls from deteriorating under the flood of late-night urinators but even the metal couldn't handle it. Rats scrabbled above her, riding the top of the lift up and down through the building. They squeaked loudly and scratched at the roof as they fought.

She had to go two flights of steps down to her family's flat; the lifts only stopped every fourth floor. The building was full of the echoing sound of the local Cantonese television station, playing a period martial arts drama at top volume in every apartment. She walked alone down the cement-floored corridor, the doors in the bare brick walls on either side barred with metal gates and small buckets of sand holding pungent incense for the door gods. Small dark shapes skittered away through the rubbish in the corners and a cat screeched somewhere nearby, barely audible over the televisions.

She reached her family's flat and opened the unlocked gate, then carefully locked it behind her; the neighbours had been robbed the week before. She was in the living room; a metre-and-a-half-wide space that took up the side of the rectangular area not partitioned off for the two miniscule bedrooms. Di Di was already asleep, lying on his side on the sofa bed next to the wall, and all the lights were off. She could easily make her way, seeing with the light from the high-rises and neon signs outside the balcony.

Ma Ma came out of the main bedroom and joined Mei as she went into her own room. She gestured for Mei to sit on the bottom bunk with her and they talked in whispers.

'You smell of blood, Mei, are you all right?' Ma Ma said.

'I'm fine, don't worry about it, it's just a scratch,' Mei said.

'What will his Nest be like? What will his mother be like?'

'If he protects you like he says he will – and he is telling the truth, I can hear it – it will be like any other house. Demons take human form, and some live on the Earth as humans. As long as they don't harm anyone, the Celestials have a treaty with

47

them to leave them alone.' She looked down at her hands. 'Unlike us foxes, who are constant targets for the Celestials.'

'I don't see why you should suffer because of something that happened hundreds of years ago!' Mei said. 'It's just not fair!'

'That's the way it works. When one of my kind does something bad, it just intensifies the prejudice. The Shen will always hate us.' She shrugged. 'We do have a capricious nature that the Shen find offensive anyway. Play one small trick on a Shen and they'll never forgive you. They're all far too serious for their own good.'

'I sometimes think it was more than one small trick, Ma Ma.'

Ma Ma's smile didn't shift. 'Maybe. But I've changed, I don't live that life any more. I'm a doctor, with a family. I help people, but the Celestials don't care, they'll still kill me on sight.' She hugged Mei again. 'With Tony's protection we'll never have to worry about the Shen. We'll all be safe.' Her smile widened. 'And he can uncurse Di Di!'

'That's the best part of all,' Mei said.

'Come to bed, old lady, stop talking to our rich daughter,' Ba Ba said, his voice full of sleep.

Di Di woke and howled.

'Oh no!' Ma Ma and Mei said in unison, and ran to stop him as he made another attempt to bash his brains out on the window bars.

The next morning Mei dragged Sandy out for a private morning tea and quizzed her.

'Did you talk to your mother about it?' Sandy waved her hand. 'No of course you didn't. Do you feel weird and guilty?'

Mei nodded.

'So it was your first time, and it was in the back of his car,' Sandy said.

Mei nodded.

Sandy smiled. 'You'd be surprised at how common it is. My first time was in a love hotel, but if he has a car then you can't blame him.'

Mei relaxed. 'Really? Because it felt…'

'Strange,' Sandy said. 'It hurts.'

48

Mei nodded.

Sandy reached across the table and took Mei's hand. 'I understand how you feel. I felt the same way after my first time, and we weren't even engaged. My sister's in London and she said that over there they have education about all of this, but for us here it's nothing except the super-awkward talk with your Ma Ma.'

Mei nodded, and wiped a tear from her eye; Sandy really did understand. 'Does it get better?'

Sandy squeezed Mei's hand. 'Oh, yes it does. He loves you, and he'll make sure it does. It won't hurt next time, and when you're accustomed to it...' She released Mei's hand and dropped her voice to a whisper. 'It becomes *wonderful*.'

'Thanks, Sandy,' Mei said, feeling much better.

'Now you need to go back to the office and make the announcement,' Sandy said. 'The gossip magazines will be all over you.' She giggled. 'You may even have paparazzi following you!'

'That's not important,' Mei said. 'The important thing is that I can be with Tony.' She sighed with bliss. 'Forever.'

Back at the office she packed up her desk. She held the little fox figurine that her mother had given her a long time ago, that had sat next to her monitor as a good luck charm.

Daniel, the only expat in the office, came past and saw her packing. 'He fired you? That's not fair, you're good at your job!'

'No, no,' Mei said.

'He asked her to marry him!' Sandy said loudly with glee.

'Congratulations,' Daniel said. 'Wait, you're going off to be a rich tai tai and have lunch and your hair done every day?' He bent to speak closely to her. 'Does that mean you'll stop dying your hair red and go back to standard black? I like the red.'

'No,' Tony said behind Daniel, and they all stepped back to make room for him. 'Even if she wasn't marrying me, I'd still promote her to CEO. And I like the red hair too.'

The other staff looked from Tony to Mei with a mixture of confusion and delight.

'Meet your new CEO, Mei Lee,' Tony said, putting one hand out towards Mei. 'She's moving into the corner office next to mine, and you all have to call her "ma'am".'

'Oh please, Tony, you're embarrassing me,' Mei said.

'Well, okay, I may be joking about the "ma'am" thing,' Tony said, and relaxed to lean on the divider. 'But you all know how well she's been managing the accounting side of things, and it's obvious she's quite capable of handling more of the administration.'

Mei waited to see whether there would be a backlash of jealousy, but instead there were quiet cheers.

'You'll be our supervisor?' Sandy said.

'I guess so, yes,' Mei said.

'Good!' Sandy said. 'Mr Kwok was ... ' She hesitated in front of the boss.

Tony finished it for her. 'An asshole. I should never have hired him. Mei will be a much better manager, she's smart and caring and you all love her.'

'Yes!' Sandy said with delight. 'I'm going to love working for you, Mei.'

'Last night I asked her family if I could marry Mei, and her father gave his permission,' Tony said, loud enough for the whole office to hear. 'I think Mei gets her charisma from her mother, her mother is truly lovely.'

'Congratulations!' Sandy said. The male employees were shaking Tony's hand and patting him on the shoulder. 'This is the best.' She turned to Tony. 'When's the wedding? You have to invite all of us!'

The rest of the staff agreed loudly and more were gathering.

'We haven't set a date yet, but don't worry, as soon as we've done the traditional boring thing for my family in China, we'll come back here and have a huge outrageously extravagant wedding banquet in one of the most expensive hotels in town,' Tony said, smiling at Mei, 'and you're all invited.'

All of the staff were gathered around her cubicle now, and everybody cheered.

'I'm overwhelmed,' Mei said.

'Back to work everybody, but meet in the lift lobby at twelve, because lunch is on me,' Tony said.

The staff wandered back to their desks, chatting loudly among themselves. Tony gave Mei a warm smile and headed back to his own office, his hands in his pockets and his stride jaunty.

'Let me help you move your stuff into your new office,' Sandy said. 'Boss.'

'You are all such good friends,' Mei said.

'That's why we're so pleased you'll be our boss,' Sandy said, and picked up one of the boxes. 'You're my best friend too.' She dropped her voice. 'We need a new CFO, Mei. Do you know who you'll promote?'

'I'll have to give it a great deal of thought,' Mei said. 'I want to be completely fair and promote the person who's best for the job.'

'Of course,' Sandy said. 'You're the boss.'

'No, Tony is, and he'll have final say,' Mei said.

'I know you'll do the right thing,' Sandy said.

They carried the boxes across the executive side, and the receptionist buzzed Mei and Sandy through. Tony was waiting for her in her new office next to his, which had windows down one wall overlooking the busy Tsim Sha Tsui street.

He handed her a key fob. 'This is for the front door of the building out of hours, the front door to the office, and the executive side. The code generator on this token is to enter the top-level banking and accounting systems.'

Sandy clapped her hands. 'Keys to the kingdom!'

'And now I need to give Mei her computer access, Sandy, so leave us,' Tony said.

Sandy nodded to them, grinning, and went out.

Tony put his hand on the computer monitor. 'Log in, you have access to everything.'

Mei sat behind the desk, the executive chair soft under her, and logged in using the number on the token. She opened the accounting program and three times as many files were present. She scrolled through them. 'Nothing from the Mainland side? RedDevil? I need to see everything about the company if I'm to manage the Hong Kong side. All of it.'

'I'll give you that access after we're married. There are employees in economically disadvantaged locations and I'm running operations that …' He searched for the word. '… bend some of the stupid government restrictions. I cut through a lot of red tape. Managing the Hong Kong side is enough for you to do anyway – you don't have to do it all.'

She turned back to the screen. 'But I could probably streamline the mainland operations like I did for Hong Kong.'

'I'll have other projects to work on after we're married, and you can take control of RedDevil then. For now, RedGold in Hong Kong is all yours.' He waved one hand at the screen. 'If you see anything you want to change, go ahead.'

'Let me run an audit, and I'll go straight to work on it.'

He kissed the top of her head. 'Don't work too hard.'

She took his hand and kissed it. 'I'm happy to be working for us.'

'You are wonderful.'

After he'd gone out, she sat and looked at the screen for a moment, then took a wild hunch and logged into the accounting software with Tony's administration ID. She tried Tony's car's registration number as the password – he had a personalised plate with many lucky eights on it – and she was in. She hesitated about going through the figures, then nodded. After they were married she'd be in control of both sides anyway.

She went through the RedDevil accounts, and concern jolted through her. There weren't any charity donations; he was giving cash gifts to his mother. There were a large number of beauty salons that he ran in Swatow – and she may have been inexperienced, but she knew what that was a code for. He employed at least thirty 'beauticians'. There were shadowy dealings that had strange, large figures running through a variety of business names that didn't seem to produce anything. Nothing she could identify as illegal, but he was right – he was bending government regulations. She needed to investigate further.

She compared RedDevil to RedGold, the Hong Kong side of the company. RedGold was squeaky clean, absolutely above-board; she'd made sure of it during her two years there. Hong Kong had an Independent Commission Against Corruption, whereas the Mainland side only had an inconsistent police force that would occasionally overlook this sort of activity. She sighed and put her chin in her hand. It still didn't sit right with her, and she wondered if there were ways for her to clean up the Mainland operation as well.

She sat straighter and delved further into the figures. She could probably bring RedDevil into line, make it legal, and even improve the profits after they were married and she had control of everything. She smiled as she launched herself into the challenge of planning the changes.

5

Mei checked her overnight bag, then placed it on her bunk. During the past two weeks she'd transferred most of her belonging's to Tony's place in preparation for her move in with him, and very little was left in her room. Ma Ma stood in the doorway, her eyes red but bright with joy.

'He's here,' Ba Ba shouted from the balcony. Mei hugged him goodbye, kissed Di Di on the cheek, then Ma Ma helped her carry her bag down to the building entrance. The big Mercedes was waiting for her, with Tony and a driver standing beside it.

The driver opened the trunk of the car and put Mei's bags in.

'Look after her,' Ma Ma said to Tony.

'She will be treated like the princess she is,' Tony said. 'Oh, I forgot.' He reached into his pocket, and pulled out a solid gold necklace, a long chain, with a bronze medallion the size of a one dollar coin hanging from it. He held it out to Ma Ma. 'Put this on your son. It will stop him from deteriorating until I return.'

Ma Ma took the chain and lifted it to study the medallion. 'It smells of demon.'

Tony put his hands in his pants pockets. 'Of course it does. I made it.'

'Oh.'

'Put it around his neck, it will protect him until I return with the curse breaker.'

'All right.' Ma Ma held her arms out, and Mei ran to her. 'Hurry back so we can have a big wedding for you, Princess Mei,' she said, holding Mei tight. 'Be careful.'

Mei pulled back. 'I will.'

Tony bowed to Ma Ma and opened the car door for Mei.

'Hello,' Mei said to the driver as Tony climbed in next to her and closed the car door. 'You're not Tony's usual driver. I don't know your name. Are you part of the company?'

'Ignore it,' Tony said as he buckled up. 'The driver, I mean. It's one of mine, a thrall. No need to talk to it, it doesn't have much of a mind. You'll meet a few of them in this trip, even though they look like people they aren't real. Don't bother talking to them, just tell them what to do. Go,' he added to the driver.

'My Lord,' the driver said, and pulled carefully away from the kerb.

Tony turned to speak to Mei. 'My Mother is at the house waiting for you. She looks quite young, but she's very, very old. Treat her with a great deal of respect. Kneel when you meet her, like she's the Empress.'

Mei nodded, intimidated.

'My other family members will be there. Don't go too close to any of them; stay next to me. Don't let any of them get you alone.'

'I understand, Tony,' Mei said, and shrunk back to make herself smaller.

He saw her face. 'It's okay, I'll protect you.' He settled more comfortably in his own seat. 'Don't break the speed limit!' he barked at the driver, making Mei jump. 'Break the speed limit one more time and you'll be dinner! There are plenty of other thralls who'd love the honour of driving me around, and don't you forget it.'

'My Lord,' the driver said, slowing.

'Mei,' he said more gently. 'My family mustn't know that I'm changing for you. They have to think that I'm still being a demon, that I'm still cruel. If they find out what you've inspired in me, they'll kill you to free me from you. Do you understand?'

Mei nodded, her eyes wide.

'I have to pretend,' he said. 'While I'm in front of them, I can't be myself.' He took her hand. 'Anything I say to you, that's selfish or cruel – just ignore it. For me. And I will make it up to you when we return home.'

'I understand, Tony,' she said, and squeezed his hand.

'You are wonderful,' he breathed, and kissed her on the cheek. 'Now I want to rest,' he said, closing his eyes. 'Tell me when we're close to the border.'

'Yes, my Lord,' the driver said, at the same time Mei said, 'Okay.'

It took most of the day as they travelled close to the city of Swatow in Chaozhou province, then followed the highway to skirt the edge of the urban area and head into the countryside. Villages of mud houses with tiled roofs dotted the landscape every two kilometres, surrounded by wandering pigs and chickens scavenging through the piles of refuse. They passed farmers walking on the road, some carrying huge loads of vegetables for market, until the driver turned off onto a gravel road and followed it through fields of mandarin trees. He went for twenty kilometres of orchard-covered hills with no farms or villages, then pulled in front of a walled compound.

'My lord,' he said softly.

Tony grunted and woke. 'Already.' He smiled at Mei. 'Let's show off my new prize. Bring the bags,' he said to the driver without looking away from her.

He climbed out of the car and strolled to the gate. Mei opened the car door and followed him. The high wall was intimidating, fitted with a groove of putty along the top filled with shards of broken glass and a double row of razor wire above that. The house on the other side wasn't visible at all.

'Hey!' Tony shouted at the gate.

The wooden doors behind the steel gate opened, and a small elderly man bowed low to Tony. 'Lord Twenty-five. Welcome home, Highness.'

'Open the damn gate!' Tony yelled.

The elderly man quickly opened the gate, then stepped back and bowed low again as Tony pushed through. Mei followed, and stopped when she was inside.

A two-storey house stood in front of her, with a traditional bracketed roof that turned up at the corners. The wooden pillars holding up the construction were painted red, and the rest of the building was dark burnished wood, glowing with age. A carefully tended garden of nearly a hectare sat around the house and was framed by the wall, with trimmed azaleas bright with flowers and a pond full of giant black koi carp.

Mei looked around; entranced; it was like a house from a fairy tale. She almost expected a Celestial fairy, wearing flowing Tang dynasty robes with long sleeves and delicate embroidery, to come floating towards them.

Tony pulled her out of her trance by grabbing her hand and leading her across a small wooden bridge that straddled the pond. 'Come on, hurry. We need to pay our respects to my Mother.' He grinned at Mei. 'You really don't want to make her angry.'

56

Mei followed him as he led her to the open double front doors of the house. A pair of stone lions stood on either side of the doors. Tony led Mei into the living room, which had stairs up to the second floor that circled the two-storey space. A massive red silk lantern hung from the ceiling, alight with electric bulbs from within to display delicate scenes of birds and flowers.

'Kneel as soon as she's down here,' Tony said, and held Mei's hand so tight it was painful.

'Is that you, Twenty-five?' a woman said, and came to the edge of the balcony to see them. 'Ah it is, and he's brought the little fox wife.'

She came down the stairs and Mei couldn't look away from her, mesmerised by her aura of cold power. Tony's mother appeared in her late thirties, not much older than Tony himself. Her shining oval face had fair smooth skin and large, luminous eyes. She wore a red old-fashioned cheongsam dress trimmed with gold. Twenty-four-carat gold chains hung from her neck and wrists, and similar gold and ruby earrings and rings decorated her ears and fingers. She glittered.

'Down. Down!' Tony whispered furiously as his mother came down the stairs, and Mei fell to one knee so quickly that she hit the bone on the floor and winced with pain. She lowered her head.

'This is the fox spirit's daughter?' Tony's mother said in front of her. Mei looked up and saw the red silk, then Tony's mother's hand was in her face. She watched the jewellery sparkle, lost for words. 'She doesn't look like much. Is her hair dyed?'

'Completely natural,' Tony said, his voice warm with pride. 'It is so good to see you, Mother.'

Tony's mother tapped Mei on her head. 'Get up child, let me see you.'

Mei pulled herself to her feet, her knee still stinging where it had hit the floor. Tony's mother grabbed her chin with one hand and moved her face from side to side, studying her. Mei was unable to move, frozen in the woman's grip.

'She looks human,' Tony's mother said. 'You'll have a battle to prevent your brother from eating her, you know what a glutton he is.'

'If he tries anything I'll kill him,' Tony said, his voice full of menace.

'You should have killed him a long time ago,' she said. She smiled knowingly at Mei's terrified expression and released her. 'Oh, you are new to all of this. This will be fun.' She waved them to a rosewood sofa in the living room and sat herself. 'Before I give my permission, I want to know what your future plans are.'

'Continue to build the business, grow our wealth, if you could provide me with more thralls the next time you hatch a clutch...'

'No!' Tony's mother waved one red-nailed hand towards Mei. 'This! I've humoured your escapades among the humans for long enough, Twenty-five. I appreciate that a fox spirit will be a good injection of intelligence and cunning into your breeding program, but you don't have a single mating Mother and you will shame our entire clan if you don't build your own Nest *now*. You must collect at least two more wives after sorting out this...' The glittering hand waved dismissively at Mei again. 'Animal, and I cannot understand why you have chosen to marry it first.'

'As soon as I have Mei settled and managing my business, I will spend all my time collecting a group of exceptionally fine Mothers and building the greatest Nest you have ever seen,' Tony said.

Mei jerked and stared at him. He nodded to her, the smile frozen on his face, and she understood; he had to pretend.

'Ah,' Tony's mother said. 'Clever boy.' She leaned forward to pat him on the knee. 'Clever boy! A capable wife who is a caretaker for the business while you build your Nest. Both sides taken care of with aplomb. Well done. I cannot wait to see which Mothers you collect, there are some very fine double-digits languishing untouched in the King's harem and ripe for defection.'

'Oh come, Mother, I know how much you'd like to see the King eat me but that's not going to happen.'

'A loving mother can always hope,' she said. She turned to Mei. 'You look completely human. Do you only eat human food?'

'She's human in every way,' Tony said before Mei could find her voice to answer. 'Her mother is a full-blood fox and her father is human.'

'We'll have to see what we can arrange for the kitchen, then,' his mother said absently. 'We may have to send one of the thralls to the market.' She focussed on Mei. 'You can cook human food, right?'

Mei bobbed her head, trying not to let Tony's mother see how much she was shaking. The woman's aura of casual violence was terrifying.

Tony's mother rose. 'Provided you have a proper Nest within the year's end, I give my approval. If you do not have a Nest with at least two fine big Mothers by New Year, I will eat this little red thing myself.'

Tony showed her upstairs and around the balcony to a bedroom with a rosewood four-poster bed and heavy wardrobe and dressing table. The thralls had already put their bags in there and Tony turned to sit on the bed.

'You like it?' he said.

She went to the window; it overlooked the garden, the high wall with its wire and glass, and the uninhabited hills beyond. 'This room is bigger than my family's whole apartment.'

'I know,' he said expansively, 'but not for long, as soon as the wedding in Hong Kong is settled, you can buy them a new place. Use the company's funds.'

She turned and leaned on the windowsill. 'Really?'

He smiled at her reaction. 'Of course.'

She sat next to him and gazed up into his eyes. 'You are so generous. I am so lucky to have you.'

He put his hand on her face and smiled down at her. 'And I'm lucky to have you. I was worried Mother would eat you on sight, but she seems quite taken with you.' He saw her expression. 'No, no, don't worry, you're perfectly safe. But you heard what she said. As soon as we're married and you're settled into running the business, I'll have to set up a Nest of my own and go hunting for a couple of Mothers, otherwise she will eat you.'

'She wouldn't, would she?' A chill ran through her. 'You can defend me.'

'She absolutely would. I can't be with you all the time, Mei. It would be best to do what she says.' He stared intensely at her. 'Is that a problem?'

'Of course it is!'

He moved away from her. 'So you want to call the wedding off? You don't love me after all?'

'Of course I love you! But I don't want to share you. I want to be your only one.'

'This is the way it is, Mei. If you can't deal with it, then I think it would be best that we call it off and I just take you home.'

She hesitated, looking at him.

He lowered his voice and fingered her gold bracelet. 'You do love me, don't you? I'd do anything for you, but if you can't do this for me then it might be best to just cancel the whole thing.'

If she left him now she'd be publicly humiliated when they returned to Hong Kong, she'd have to leave her job and her brother would never be restored. Or his mother might eat her anyway…

'She's dangerous and powerful,' Tony said, as if he'd read her mind. 'I have to do as she says.' He took her hand. 'I don't want to find other wives, but I have to.' He shook his head, full of remorse. 'If you love me you'll do this for me, and I will be forever grateful. Help me, Mei.'

She took a deep breath to argue, and realised – he was right. If she truly loved him, she would accept him the way he was, demon and everything. She could make him a better person, and help him to see that she was all he needed. She just had to get him back to Hong Kong and start their lives together. She could change him.

'All right.' She kissed his hand. 'Don't worry about the business, I'll look after everything for you. You just do what you need to do.'

'I knew I could count on you. You make me so happy.' He leaned to whisper in her ear. 'I'm going to take her down one day and replace her with a Mother of my own.' He moved closer and nuzzled her ear, moving his mouth down the side of her neck. He eased her suit jacket open to run his hands over her breasts. 'Thank you so much.'

She shivered with desire, wanting to try the lovemaking again, aching for the intimacy with her love. She slid her hand down his chest and to his crotch, and his breath quickened.

'You'll see that you don't need more than me,' she said.

'You're right, you're always right,' he said. 'You make me a better man.'

She pushed her hand into him and his eyes glazed over with pleasure. 'I will do anything it takes to keep you with me.' She undid his pants and took him in her hand, gently stroking him. 'If you need more wives, then I'll look after everything while you go find them.' And, she added to herself, make sure that you want me more.

'You ... are ... wonderful,' he said.

'Only the best for you, my love,' she said.

He pushed her onto her back, still thrusting into her hand, and undid the buttons of her blouse. He shoved his face between her breasts. 'Lose the clothes,' he said.

'I have to let go of you,' she said.

He pulled away, stood, and dropped his pants to the floor. He pointed at her. 'Clothes. Off. Now.' He started to undo the buttons on his shirt.

She stood and took off her suit jacket, crumpled and askew on top of her gaping blouse. She threw it onto the bed behind her, then undid the rest of the buttons and tossed the blouse there as well. He was naked in front of her – tanned, strong and muscular, and stroked himself as he watched her undress.

'Bra,' he said. She looked him coyly in the eye as she unclipped it and tossed it onto the bed as well.

'Touch them,' he said, his eyes dark with desire.

She'd show him that she was the best. She wiggled in her skirt, ran her hands up her sides and over her breasts, and squeezed her nipples. She threw her head back with pleasure.

'Nice,' he said. 'Leave the skirt but take your panties off. I like the skirt, very woman-in-control.'

'I want you in control,' she said as she slipped her hands under the skirt and pulled her panties off, then tossed them onto the bed as well.

He took a step forward, pushed her back to lie on the bed, and slid her skirt high over her thighs, raising her legs so she was in position.

'My little pet dog,' he said.

'I'm not a ...' she began, but he shoved himself into her and she lost her voice.

He did it hard and rough and bit her nipples until she squealed with pain, and she tried to push him away.

'Tony, you're hurting me,' she said.

He glared into her face, the demonic scent rising from him. 'If you love me you'll accept me for what I am. I'm a demon, and it will sometimes hurt.' He shoved into her again. 'I'll try to control myself, but you drive me wild.'

'Just don't hurt me,' she said.

'Love is pain,' he said, and bit her again.

Her yelps of pain sent him over the edge and he stared into her face, fierce and restrained, as he spent himself inside her.

When he was done and had fallen beside her on the bed, he smiled and gently touched her cheek. 'I'm sorry I hurt you, I lost control,' he said softly. 'With your help, I can control the cruelty. Just put up with me while I learn, okay?'

She smiled back through the tears. 'All right.'

She moved closer to hold him, seeking reassurance, but he pushed her away and rose.

'The rest of the family will be here for dinner soon.' He turned back and studied her half-naked form. 'I like the skirt, keep it on for the rest of the day.'

She rose as well and picked up her clothes. 'I'm looking forward to meeting them over dinner.'

'You won't. It's not your sort of food,' he said.

'Oh,' she said.

'I suppose we'll have to find some human food for you before everybody else arrives,' he said. 'What a nuisance. Hurry up and get dressed, and we'll see what we can arrange.'

Tony came into the kitchen as she boiled the noodles and fish that the thralls had found for her at the market. The aroma made her dizzy with hunger; she'd had a piece of bread before leaving home that morning and nothing else all day. Tony didn't seem to eat nearly as much as she did, and she'd need to find a way to work around it.

'We're ready to eat now,' he said. 'You have to go up to the room and eat there.'

'I understand,' she said, and poured the soup out of the wok into a bowl. She grabbed some chopsticks and a spoon as he waited impatiently, then nodded to him. 'I'm done.'

'Stay close,' he said, and opened the kitchen door. It led into the passage under the stairs, and he took her carefully through a door into the entry hall so she could go up.

'Close your eyes,' he said, and she obliged. He took her by the upper arm and she hoped the precious food wasn't spilling as he led her.

'Step up,' he said.

Someone whimpered behind her and she shivered. She carefully nudged the step with her foot and went up. The air filled with the foul smell of demon essence; the house was full of demons. She thought of his mother, powerful and cruel, and it sent a chill through her.

'Keep going up,' he said, nudging her. 'Don't look.'

'Idiot,' a man said with a mouth full of food behind and below her, making her jump. 'She has to learn eventually.'

There was a loud crunching sound, like a bone being crushed, and she squeaked. The chills increased and she shivered again. She felt like an antelope with a pride of hungry lions staring hungrily at her back, and she opened her eyes to see where she was on the stairs to make a run for the top.

'Don't look!' Tony said. 'Top of the stairs here. Just walk now.'

Wet tearing echoed from below her, and more bones crunching. The prey feeling intensified, and she wanted to run more than anything. Her eyes filled with tears of terror as she shuffled forward and she heard him open the door. He led her into the room, away from the smell of demon. The air filled with the scent of her clean clothing, his sharp cruel essence, and the sexual aftermath on the bed.

'All right,' he said. 'You can open your eyes now. You spilled half of that on the stairs, you'll have to clean it up later. Now lock the door and don't let anyone in but me. Eat something and don't come down until I tell you.'

'Tony...?' she said as she placed the noodles on the dressing table. The smell didn't make her hungry any more, instead she felt slightly sick.

'What?'

She turned to face him. 'Will you eat like this when we're married? I've always seen you eating human food.'

He smiled. 'I really prefer this way. Human food is interesting, but this is much more satisfying. Once I've destroyed the maids and moved you into my house, I plan to eat this way as often as I can.' His face twisted with impatience. 'Anything else you want to bother me with? I'm starving and they're eating them all.'

'No, no,' she said, and bobbed her head. 'I just want to make sure you're comfortable after we're married. You go. Eat.'

'Good,' he said, went out and closed the door behind him.

Someone screamed downstairs and there was loud, cruel laughter. She went to the door and locked it. A crash resonated through the house and she flinched. She hesitated, listening, but all the sounds were coming from downstairs. She'd hear them if they came up the stairs for her. If they came to the door, she could jump out the window, but she probably wouldn't outrun them. The fence was too high to go over anyway, and the gate was locked. She had to rely on Tony's protection.

She leaned on the door and thought of her family, squeezed into that tiny apartment, and her brother living a nothing-life in his wheelchair, unaware of his precious young years bleeding away. She went back to the dressing table and sat in front of the noodles, looking at them for a long time.

She needed to eat, and stay strong, and survive the wedding, so she could return home and take control of the business, buy the family a new place to live, and free her brother. Tony's mother had said that Mei was a welcome member of the clan. She had to trust that her value as a business partner was important to them. More important than her value as food, anyway. Tony loved her, and he would protect her.

The top of the noodles rippled as another crash reverberated through the house, followed by a series of terrified inhuman screams. She picked up her spoon and chopsticks and dug into the food.

After she ate she crawled onto the bed, fully-clothed, and curled up with misery hugging a pillow. She hadn't expected so much ... evil. She was stuck in the middle of nowhere and had to trust Tony to keep her alive. She understood now – when her mother had said he loved her, it was "whatever they considered love". He loved her, but he would still hurt her, and be unfaithful to her. The only advantage was that she would take control of the company and could build a better life for her family.

She just had to survive long enough to return to Hong Kong and get the final marriage certificate from the government, and make it legal. She searched her heart; she really did love him and didn't want to leave him. She would try her best to teach him to be a better man. She sighed into the pillow and wiped her eyes with it. At least her family would be free when he uncursed Di Di; and if Tony couldn't do it she could save up her executive salary and pay the schoolgirl.

And if he didn't change his ways, then he would be off making his Nest and having the violent sex with the other wives and probably leave her alone. Once they were married back in Hong Kong she would have the government paperwork done, and legally be his wife. As long as she ran the business and was a loyal wife, he had no reason to hurt her, and wouldn't be around much. Whatever happened, her family would have a better life.

If she tried to leave him the result would probably be lethal, anyway. She knew too much.

She nodded to herself. Whether he changed or not, she would survive and take control of the company and make sure that her family were cared for.

He tapped on the door. 'Mei?'

She shot upright, checked her clothes and hair, and went to open the door for him. He smiled through the opening and her heart lifted to see him. She should never have doubted him; everything would be all right as long as she was with him.

'We've finished eating and it's safe for you to come down now. Come and meet the family,' he said.

'Do I look all right?' she said, turning to check herself in a mirror and finding no mirrors at all.

'You look fine. Come on.' He grabbed her hand. 'They're waiting to meet you.'

'Should I kneel again?' she whispered to him as he led her around the balcony. The rest of his family were visible below, watching them with curiosity.

'Good idea,' he said. 'You don't have to, but it will make her happy.'

'I want to make all of you happy,' she said, trying to keep the fear from her voice.

He squeezed her hand.

They walked down the stairs holding hands, the faces of his family shining up at her. At the bottom of the stairs they all stood under the huge silk lantern lighting the entry hall. The other rooms in the mansion were dark, and echoes of sound came from the kitchen at the back of the house. She went to Tony's mother and knelt on the polished floorboards in front of her. 'Lady.'

'Good girl.'

Mei rose and looked around at the people who had arrived while she'd been cooking the 'human' food. A man and a woman stood under the lantern; the man appeared similar to Tony except with blond dyed hair, and he was accompanied by an elegant woman who looked south east Asian – Thai or Vietnamese. They were both wearing silk business suits, him in grey and her in navy.

'This is Mei, my fox spirit,' Tony said expansively. 'Mei, this is – ' He gestured towards the blond man. 'My brother, uh...'

'Wang,' Wang said, shaking Mei's hand and moving far too close into her personal space. He towered over her and leered into her eyes, making her shrink back. 'I love the red hair.' He turned and gestured towards the suited woman. 'My sister, Chung.'

Chung nodded to Mei, serious, then grimaced at Wang. 'Back off.'

Wang leaned into Mei's ear and spoke in a theatrical whisper that was much too loud for her sensitive hearing, filling her nose with the foul scent of demon. 'Don't mind her, she's just jealous.'

'So am I,' Tony growled.

Wang's grin widened as he ran his hand down Mei's side and cupped her behind. She resisted the urge to shake him off and back away, revolted by his greedy leer. She knew better than to appear weak to them.

'Back. Off,' Tony said, a low snarl of threat.

66

Wang released her, still leering, and stepped back to stand next to Chung. She elbowed him in the ribs, and he ignored her. 'Delighted.'

Mei bowed slightly to him. 'I am honoured to meet you.'

'Good girl,' Tony's mother said. 'Come and sit, and tell us all about yourself. You're marrying into the clan tomorrow, and we want to know everything about you.'

They went into the living room, and the room's central light brightened as they entered. The entry lantern faded, again leaving the rest of the house in darkness. Everybody stood and waited as Tony's mother sat in one of the armchairs in the pool of light at the centre of the room. Tony sat in the other chair, the other couple sat on the sofa, so Mei sat on the rug next to Tony's feet, curling her legs under her. He patted her on the head, then stroked her hair, and she felt a flush of satisfaction. If she did this right, and pleased them all, she'd be safe and clear to return home.

'So how much is this business in Hong Kong worth?' Wang asked.

'No idea, Mei handles the numbers,' Tony said. 'Mei?'

'Gross income of seventy-five million US last financial year,' Mei said.

'Oh, that's just the business that goes through the accounting section,' Tony said dismissively. 'A large number of the transactions are off-the-books, and Mei hasn't taken control of them yet.' He smiled down at her. 'She'll be in charge of everything after we're married.'

'I can't wait,' she said with enthusiasm.

'You are a little treasure,' Tony's mother said.

Mei relaxed slightly and leaned on Tony's leg.

'She's good with accounts? I could use her, she's very cute. How much?' Wang said, and his sister beamed.

'Not for sale, and she's being promoted from accounting manager to general manager when we're back home,' Tony said with pride.

'Do you have a brother or sister?' Wang asked Mei.

Mei tried to keep smiling.

'Oh, that's a very sad story,' Tony said, still jovial. 'Her only brother inherited the fox nature, but he's been cursed. He has the mind of a three-year-old and he's stuck in a wheelchair, can't use his arms or legs. Very sad.'

'They bring it on themselves, I suppose,' Tony's mother said. 'Foxes are always capricious and spiteful.'

Mei opened her mouth and took a deep breath, then let the breath out and closed her mouth.

'Speak, little one,' Tony's mother said with amusement.

'I was going to say, that you are so right,' Mei said. 'He did it to himself, he failed in his job and deserved everything he received.'

Tony's mother looked piercingly at her, probably seeing the lie. Then she smiled. 'You will fit into our family very well, Little Red.'

'I like that. Little Red,' Wang said. 'I think I'll call you that.' His expression grew hungry. 'Is your blood as red as your hair?'

Mei went cold again, and shivered.

'Thirty-four,' Tony growled, not noticing her reaction.

Wang leaned back and raised his hands. 'Sorry, sorry.'

'You've eaten enough, you don't need to eat another thing,' Tony's mother said. 'You'll grow fat eating like that. Pig. I won't have enough thralls left to keep my garden tidy.'

'Then get humans,' Wang said. 'They taste better anyway.'

She stabbed her finger at him. 'You do that and I will eat you myself, Thirty-four. I've had to pay off the police so many times that I'm running out of money.'

'I'll send you some money, Mother,' Tony said. 'Just tell me when you need funds, you know I have plenty.'

'See? That is why you are the best son,' Tony's mother said. 'Now I am tired. We have the wedding tomorrow, and it must happen before noon. So get some sleep, and we will all gather here tomorrow morning and see our beloved Twenty-five finally gain a wife, even if it is only a dog.'

The rest of the family rose and bowed to her. Mei stood, then fell to one knee and lowered her head.

'You will fit in very well,' Tony's mother said absently as she touched Mei's head in passing.

6

The next morning Tony left her alone to dress as the family set the wedding up. It was difficult putting the wedding dress on without a mirror, but at least her makeup had small mirrors in the compacts. Her breasts were covered in Tony's bites from the lovemaking, making them sore, but he hadn't drawn blood.

It was hard to get the lipstick right when she was smiling with relief. They'd return to Hong Kong that afternoon, directly after the wedding, and things would return to normal. Everything would be all right.

She did a final inspection of her face and hair, smoothed down the red silk dress with the dragon and phoenix embroidered in gold and silver thread, then opened the door to go down.

Everybody made loud sounds of appreciation as she descended the stairs.

'So beautiful,' Wang said. 'You sure you won't part with her?'

'Not for a billion US,' Tony said. His face was alight as he held his hand out for her. She went to him and took his hand, and he raised it to his face and kissed it. 'You are one of a kind,' he said softly.

'Thank you,' she said.

The rosewood sofas had been pulled to the sides to make space, and the dining table was set up under the family altar. The altar was bigger than the usual nook box; it was a full cupboard hung on the wall, a metre and a half wide and a metre high, holding statues and tablets for generations of the ancestors. Mei hesitated when she saw that the statues weren't the Taoist deities and the Buddha; they were demons.

Demon Dukes, human-shaped men with the heads of bulls and horses, held weapons impaling human babies. In the centre stood the King of the Demons himself, a blood-red snake back end with a human front end. Snake Mothers flanked him on their serpent coils, their skinless human front ends holding women writhing in terror. She made the connection and glanced at Tony's mother – that was why they used the capital M when they spoke of her. She was a Snake Mother, one of the most vicious and sadistic types of demon. Mei had only heard of them in passing; they weren't common, but when Ma Ma spoke of them she dropped her voice as if even mentioning them would make one appear.

On the silk-decked table below the altar sat a boiled pig's head with red paper draped over it, together with fragrant incense candles and small cups of red offering wine. She hesitated when the smell hit her – it wasn't wine, it was blood. She pushed the nausea down.

She stood side-by-side with Tony in front of the altar, and all Tony's family were full of pride as they bowed to the altar and paid their respects to the previous generations and the Demon King. Wang's sister Chung handed Mei a tray with cups of dark liquid on it. She panicked for a moment, then saw they were just tea. Tony's mother sat on one of the sofas, and Mei went to her, knelt, and held the tray out.

Tony's mother took a cup of tea and sipped it, then returned the cup to the tray. Before Mei could move, Tony's mother reached to grab Mei's wrist where she held the tray, and clasped it firmly. Her skin was as cold as a dead thing's. Mei froze, desperately hoping that Tony would protect her.

'You must call me Mother now,' she said.

Mei bowed her head to hide her expression, but her trembling voice gave her away. 'Mother.'

Tony's mother smiled with encouragement. 'Good girl.'

Mei rose and put the tray on the table. Tony held his arms out and she fell into them. He held her close, brushing his hand over her hair, and everybody applauded.

There was a crash and a scream, and Tony released her. He exploded into a gush of black foul-smelling liquid that sprayed over her face and dress. There were more screams and crashes around her but her eyes were full of the black goo and she couldn't see. She fell back and frantically wiped at her streaming eyes. People moved through the blurry tears, and more black liquid flew through the air. She screamed when she realised what was happening. Not now. Not *now*. Not before the marriage was legal, not before Di Di was uncursed! Something smacked into her side and she slammed into a wall, breaking everything inside her. She fell onto the floor in a haze of agony.

'Don't kill the bride she's human!' a man shouted, and she was grabbed by the upper arm and dragged into the garden, causing her so much pain with the movement that she screamed again. Cold water was splashed over her and the shock of it stopped her screaming. It cleared her eyes and she could see; a big Chinese man with white hair and huge sideburns, wearing traditional armour, was holding her arm with one hand and a blackened sword with the other. She recognised him: it was the White Tiger god, the same one who'd chased Ma Ma in Causeway Bay. She tried to rise and couldn't; then saw her legs. Blood, and the bone sticking out ...

She wanted to vomit but her eyes were full of raging darkness and everything went black.

7

Mei opened her eyes and saw a plain white ceiling with a rail and curtain on it, like a hospital. She looked left and into the brown eyes of a Chinese woman in her mid-forties with a kind face. Mei tried to pull herself upright but the woman put her hand on Mei's arm to stop her.

'Lie still and get your bearings. You have two broken legs and internal injuries and you can't move yet,' the woman said in Hong Kong-accented Cantonese.

Mei was aware of the pain from her legs but it seemed to be happening to someone else. In fact everything seemed to be happening to someone else. Her head was fuzzy and she was very sleepy …

'Have I been drugged?' she said, and heard her voice slurring.

'Strong painkillers. Let us know if it hurts too much.'

Mei noticed the drip in her arm, but didn't care. Then she remembered what had happened and everything snapped into focus. She was in a single hospital room, with a large window covered by beige curtains. The bed was a standard hospital bed – ports for oxygen and a light were above her head.

'Is Tony okay?' she said.

'Don't worry about anyone. Just rest and get better.'

'No.' Mei tried to get out of bed and the woman held her again. 'I have to find Tony. We were getting married. What day is it? We have to be in the registry office in Hong Kong the day after the wedding in China. I have to marry Tony. Everything depends on it.' She struggled to get out of bed and the woman held her more strongly.

'Get the Tiger,' the woman said.

'I need to be with Tony!' Mei said, pushing her hand off.

'Tony's dead,' a male voice said at the entrance to the room. It was the same white-haired warrior – the White Tiger God. A Shen. All she needed.

Mei fell back. 'No. Don't kill Tony, I love him.'

'I understand that this is scary but there are a few things you need to know,' the Tiger God said, gruff. 'You don't know what you were involved in. He was a very evil man and we had to destroy him.'

'You killed him?' Mei said.

'They were evil. They were...' He hesitated. 'They were demons. As soon as you're better we'll explain everything and take you home.'

Tony was dead. The love of her life was gone. She glared up at the Tiger, her eyes flooding with tears.

He moved so fast he was invisible, grabbed her wrist, and yanked it. She yelped and pulled her arm back. He raised his hand, holding the bracelet, and everything snapped into focus. It was like a cloud lifted from over her head, and she took a few deep breaths.

'What...' she said.

He studied the bracelet as it hung from his fingers. 'Cursed.' He sniffed it. 'Love curse. That bastard forced you to love him.' He flipped it through his fingers. 'There's something else there, too, something that affects free will. He kept you in love and in his control.'

Her head cleared. He'd been cruel to her, he'd hurt her, and he was going to find other wives... and she'd put up with it all. She would never let anyone treat her like that... the bracelet. It had kept her in love with him. How had she ever thought she could change him? What she'd seen at his mother's house was the real Tony – a savage demon who ate people and cared nothing for others. He'd lied to her, controlled her, and hurt her.

And now he was dead, and she was left with nothing. They hadn't completed the legal wedding ceremony back in Hong Kong, and they weren't officially married.

'It wasn't legal yet,' she said. The consequences flooded through her and she glared up at the Tiger. 'You killed Tony just before the marriage was legal!'

'He was a demon.'

'I know that!' Mei cried. 'Who are you people?'

'I'm the Emperor of the Western Heavens, the White Tiger,' he said. 'This is my palace, and this is one of my wives, Fion.'

'*One* of your wives?'

Fion smiled. 'I'm from Hong Kong too.'

'How do you know about demons and Shen?' he said.

Mei shook her head.

'You're a demon as well?' he said. 'Part-demon? That hair looks naturally red, not dyed. What are you?'

'I'm nothing special! Keep away from me. I just want to go home to my family!' She started to sob again. 'Oh god, my family!'

'It takes a special type of desperation to marry a demon when you know what it is. That one had a massive criminal empire. People were disappearing for ten li around that house.'

Mei nodded.

'You knew?'

Mei saw herself being accused of complicity with Tony's dealings. She remained silent.

The Tiger levered himself off the wall. 'Don't worry, it doesn't matter what you did – you're human and I'm sworn to protect you. Even if you were a part of the business, I can't do anything about it. I just want to know how you knew he was a demon.'

'He told me,' Mei said.

The Tiger grunted. 'Good try. Tell me the truth.'

Mei lowered her head and couldn't stop the whimper that escaped her.

'She's terrified. Leave her alone,' Fion said.

'I vow I will not harm you. Tell me why you fear,' the Tiger said.

Mei shook her head, silent. Anything should told the Celestial could mean a swift death sentence for a fox child like her, particularly one that had been consorting with demons.

'You can trust us, Mei,' Fion said gently. 'He's vowed not to hurt you, and he means it.'

Mei sniffled and grabbed another tissue. 'Where am I? Am I in Swatow?'

'You're in the Tiger's palace in the Western Heavens,' Fion said.

'I'm a prisoner in the Heavens?'

'No, of course not,' Fion said. 'As soon as you're well enough, we'll take you home.' She hesitated, then said, 'If you're in trouble we can help you.'

'You're the reason I'm in trouble!' Mei said. She wanted to turn away from Fion but couldn't with the broken legs. 'I

74

need to tell my family I'm alive. Can I use the phone?' She hesitated. 'Do you have phones?'

'I'll bring you one.'

Mei relaxed back onto the bed. 'Thank you.' At least she'd be able to tell her family that she was alive; they'd be worried about her. The thought of breaking the news about Di Di made the tears flow again. She wiped her face with the tissues, rested her sore head on the sodden pillow, and stopped fighting the drug-induced sleep.

Mei jerked awake; someone had shoved something cold against her arm. She tried to pull herself upright, then remembered that her legs were in plaster. She raised her arm to see what it was, and froze. A pair of bright blue eyes in a green scaled face below a pair of horns very similar to a deer's horns...

'Sorry, I didn't mean to wake you,' the dragon said with a woman's voice. It was two metres long and covered in green scales, with a blue fin on its tail. It snuffed at her arm. 'You smell human.'

Mei lay with her mouth open, too stunned to move.

'What are you doing with my patient, Lady Fion?' a man said from the door way. Mei looked to the door and felt another jolt of shock; it was a man in a doctor's white coat – with the head of a lion, shaggy mane and all. She rubbed her eyes, and he was still there.

'The Tiger asked me to check if she's human,' the dragon said.

The lion-headed man came in, lowered his head towards Mei, and sniffed her.

Mei jerked her arm back. 'Stop smelling me!'

'Some sort of dog?' the lion-headed man said. 'I don't know. Something exotic, but not human.'

'This is insane!' Mei said.

'Sorry, I never introduced myself, you were heavily sedated when I set your legs.' the lion-headed man said. 'I'm Doctor Bai. It would make things much easier if you told me now whether you're human or not.'

'I'm one hundred per cent human!' Mei said, not believing she was having this argument. 'Why do you have the head of a lion?'

75

'Do I?' Doctor Bai said, and touched his nose. 'Oh, yes, I do too.' He concentrated, twisting his mouth into strange shapes, and changed to a Chinese man in his mid-fifties. 'There we are. I lose the shape sometimes. May I examine you? I need to check your circulation, to ensure that your legs heal well. You had some internal injuries as well.'

Mei nodded, and he pulled the sheet back to inspect her feet.

'I smell her as human,' the dragon said. 'Maybe she owns a pet or something?'

'My brother's a vet,' Mei said, still bewildered at having to explain herself to a dragon and a lion. 'He occasionally cares for rescued wildlife.'

The dragon nodded. 'That's it then.' She hoisted herself onto her hind legs and changed back to Fion. She handed Mei a phone. 'This is for you, you said you needed to call your family.'

Mei took the phone. 'Thank you.' She studied Fion. 'So you're a dragon?'

Fion nodded, her round cheeks plump with her smile, then turned and pulled the curtains back from the window, revealing brilliant deep blue sky without a single cloud. The window was too small to show more than the intensely blue sky, but the sunlight hit the wall and it was either morning or evening. Mei checked the clock on the wall; 8 am. Morning. She'd slept the whole night.

'You're a dragon married to a tiger,' Mei said.

Fion turned back to her and nodded, still smiling.

Mei studied the doctor. 'And you're a lion.'

'The Tiger is my father,' Doctor Bai said. 'I see,' the doctor said. He palpated her abdomen over her hospital gown. 'Does this hurt?'

'No,' Mei said.

'Good.' He pulled the sheet back over her. 'Your legs will be itchy but it's important not to scratch inside the plaster. You should be out of here in six weeks or so.'

'You're a lion, and your father is a tiger?' Mei said, even more confused.

Bai nodded. 'My mother's a human. She's very proud of me.'

'She's not your mother?' Mei said, gesturing towards Fion, who didn't seem bothered.

Fion shrugged. 'My husband has many wives. It's just the way he is.'

'This is a zoo,' Mei said, almost to herself.

'Call home,' Fion said. 'I'll be back later with some novels for you to read. What do you like?'

'Anything,' Mei said.

Fion nodded. 'I'll see what I can find.'

'She's right you know,' Bai said, his face drifting to be half-human, half-lion. 'This is a zoo.'

'Wouldn't want it any other way,' Fion said. She retook dragon form, jumped a metre off the floor, and floated out of the room, writhing through the air.

'Rest and let yourself heal. We'll look after you,' the doctor said. He pointed at a button on a long cable. 'Press that if you need anything.' He went out and closed the door.

Mei studied the button, full of indecision. She did need something – she'd just woken and her bladder was achingly full – and there was no way she could make it into the bathroom by herself. She closed her eyes, screwed up her courage, and pressed the button.

Two minutes later a cheerful young woman – reassuringly human – came in and stopped. 'Are you all right? What do you need?'

'Uh…' Mei could feel herself blushing. 'I can't make it to the bathroom by myself.'

The woman became even more cheerful. 'I will help you. Just wait one moment!' She nearly jumped with delight and scurried out of the ward, returning quickly with a bedpan. 'Don't worry, I'm a tree spirit and stronger than an average human, I'll have no trouble lifting you. Let's close the door and make sure you're comfortable, and then I'll bring you breakfast.'

When she woke again the sun was high in the sky and a phone was on her bedside table. She grabbed it and called Sandy.

'Sandy Zhou.'

'Sandy. Thank God.'

'Mei! What happened? We all went to the hotel for the wedding banquet, and you weren't there. We tried to call you and Tony, and there was no answer. Are you okay? You weren't kidnapped or anything, were you? Because the police are here looking for you.'

Mei had her speech already prepared. 'I'm fine. There was an accident. I'm in hospital, and Tony's here with me. Could you tell my family and the police for me? Just tell them we're all right and we'll be home as soon as we can.'

'Tony's there? Can I speak to him?'

'He's asleep, he was injured as well. We were in a car accident. Both my legs were injured –'

'Oh, how awful!'

'And Tony has head injuries. We're both recovering and we'll be back as soon as we can, so tell my family I'm okay –'

'I'm on my way right now,' she said, determined. 'Which hospital?'

'No, Sandy, we need you and KP Poon to stay there and mind the business until we return. The doctors say it will be a few weeks, so look after it until we can come home.'

'What's your number?'

'I'll text it to you as soon as I know it,' Mei said. 'This is a borrowed phone.'

'I see.' Her voice softened. 'Hey, you just concentrate on getting better, okay? And tell Tony we're all cheering for him to get better too. We'll look after things until you're back. It's strange though …'

'What's strange?'

'Well, the police aren't just worried about you being missing. They're investigating the business.'

Mei's heart went cold. 'Have they said what they're looking for?'

'They said they had a tipoff, about prostitution and protection money and money laundering – it's ludicrous. I told them we're not involved in any of that, we're a trading firm, but they won't listen and they're going through all the files right now.'

'Don't tell them that I contacted you, they'll come after us and Tony isn't well enough to handle an interrogation. I'll fix everything up when I'm back home.'

78

'Okay, if you so say so. How long do you think it will take?'

Fortunately Mei had inherited some of her mothers' healing ability. 'Not more than a couple of weeks. Stall them until I get there, okay?'

'For a couple of weeks? Mei, this is the *police*.'

'Don't tell them you spoke to me. Let us stay missing for now while I sort something out.'

'Whatever you say.'

'Thanks Sandy. Bye.' Mei hung up. At least her family would know she was safe. But she may not have a company to go back to if the police were in there first. She looked at the plaster covering her legs. If the police found out the extent of Tony's criminal activities on the Mainland she could be returning to a jail cell.

Fion was sitting beside the bed when Mei woke again. The light in the window was fading; the day had passed while Mei had slept.

'You set the police on them,' Mei said.

'We had to,' Fion said. 'The criminal empire needed to be closed down. He had prostitutes working for him.'

'I know that,' Mei said. 'I know the name and location of every single one of them.'

'And you let it happen?'

'I was planning to set up a factory, making designer sunglasses. In Swatow,' Mei said, smiling at the irony. 'I was going to close down the brothels and free them all the minute we were married and I had greater control. I would give them worthwhile jobs in the factory, a few of them were bright enough to be promoted to management with a little mentoring. Most of them wanted to study and further themselves, and I was in the process of creating a fund for them. He had no idea.' Her smile disappeared. 'Now it's been shut down and they'll have nothing. I hope they don't end up in jail, they had no other choice.'

'I see,' Fion said.

'Did the police find the illegal side of RedGold?' Mei said. 'He kept the two sides of the business completely separate, so he'd still have the legal revenue if the illegal part was raided. Did they find anything?'

'They haven't gone very far with their investigation, but my husband led a team to shut down all the brothels and protection gangsters anyway.'

'He didn't hurt any of the girls did he?' Mei said, struggling to sit up and failing. 'They never did anything wrong, they were just trying to provide for their families!'

'He won't hurt them. He'll free them and gave them worthwhile jobs in a factory he owns in Guangzhou. The management team there are excellent and will look after them.'

'With his own men running it, because a bunch of worthless whores couldn't possibly have any brains or potential.'

Fion deliberately changed the subject. 'You've been telling the staff in the company that Tony's alive.'

'Of course I have.' If the authorities in Hong Kong discovered that Tony was dead, they'd close the company and all the employees would lose their jobs. It needed to stay running long enough for Mei to ensure everybody was taken care of.

'You haven't called your family directly, only left messages for them through the company.'

Mei didn't repeat herself. She had to protect her mother and brother from the Celestials.

'You knew exactly what he was. Why did you stay with him?'

'He put that bracelet on me – he was controlling me. Your husband has multiple wives. Why do you stay with *him*?'

She winced. 'We know. We're trying to teach him about modern women's rights.'

'You're not getting very far, if you're just one of his *many* wives.'

Fion made a soft sound of frustration and went out. Mei turned towards the window and brushed the tears away. The crystalline blue sky was fading in the afternoon sun, and a green and blue dragon – probably Fion – flew past. Mei watched it, enthralled for a moment by its effortless freedom, then turned to her bedside table and picked up one of the romance novels that Fion had left for her.

'RedGold, Sandy speaking.'

'Sandy, it's Mei.'

'Mei. How's Tony? It's a week already, please come home, we can't do this without you!'

'I'm hoping to be out of here soon, but Tony's still very unwell. He may not be able to return to work for a while.'

'That's great about you, but is he really that bad?'

'I think it will be a long time before he's well enough to take over again.'

'That's such a shame! It's awful that this happened right as you were getting married.'

'This is what marriage is about, right? Sticking together? I'm sticking with him and looking after him, and I'll have him back home in Hong Kong soon.'

'Good, we really need you here!'

'So, are the police still going through everything?'

'They didn't find anything illegal, which isn't surprising. They yelled at us for a long time to give them your number or the number of the hospital, and then they suddenly just stopped and left us alone. But I have a dozen invoices here and I don't know what to do with them, and some of our contractors have issues with their salaries, and I really need you here!'

The Tiger came into the room and stopped next to the doorway.

'I have to go,' Mei said. 'I'll call you back later.'

'Come home soon!' Sandy shouted as Mei hung up and placed the phone next to the stack of romance novels Fion had brought her.

The Tiger bent from the waist and held one hand out, palm-up. 'May I?'

Mei gestured for him to enter.

He came in and sat in the chair next to her bed. He was considerably bigger than Tony; strong and muscular, with a golden face framed by white sideburns. His white hair was shaggy and wild, and his eyes were pale gold. His musky scent was pure big cat, but overlaid on that was the sweeter essence of a Celestial Shen of Heaven, something that Mei rarely smelled. He glowed golden in her sight; a pure and divine power that made Tony small, dark and vicious by comparison.

'They tell me you're coming along nicely,' he said. 'Are you well enough to talk?'

She nodded.

'How much do you know about us?' he said. 'Do you know who I am?'

'You're the White Tiger of the West?'

'That's right.'

'You don't look like a tiger.'

'I can take tiger form if you want to see. I have many forms.' He smiled. 'Some of my wives really like the fur.'

'Old women curse you, and bang an effigy of you with a shoe under the overpass in Causeway Bay,' she said.

He leaned one elbow on the arm of his chair and hid the smile behind his hand. 'It's a living for them, I suppose.' He straightened and dropped his hand to concentrate on her. 'You told Fion that you were planning to reassign the sex workers in your husband's brothels, and give them something more worthwhile to do.'

She looked him in the eye. 'I was.'

'So before he put that bracelet on you – how did you get involved with the demon in the first place?'

She hesitated, trying to work out a truth that would satisfy him: she couldn't mention her mother or brother's special nature. Celestials could see through any lie.

He saw her hesitation. 'Did he abuse you?'

'He never beat me up,' she said.

'That's not what I asked.' He leaned forward to study her, his cat-gold eyes full of compassion. 'Was he abusing you?'

She hesitated again.

'Well?' he said.

'Define "abuse",' she said.

He turned away, exasperated. 'Stupid question, he was a demon. Of course he was. Look.' He turned back and reached to take her hand, and she pulled away from him. 'You can stay as long as you like, you're safe from the demons here. I can bring your family up here as well, you told Fion that your brother is disabled and you needed the marriage to pay for his treatment. I may be able to provide him with a Celestial remedy for whatever ails him.' His voice softened and his expression filled with such genuine sympathy that it made Mei's heart ache. 'Let me help you.'

She didn't allow herself to imagine what it would be like to be helped by a strong Celestial. The Tiger's noble essence glowed with perfect compassion; he would sincerely care for her – Mei's mother had told her that all Celestials had made a vow to protect humans. But foxes were a different matter – he'd probably kill her mother on sight.

He continued, his voice warm with kindness. 'Would you like to work with the prostitutes, and finish what you started? I have extensive business dealings on the Earthly, Mei – similar to your boy Tony's but with a focus on promoting social justice – and could always use a good accountant, particularly one as completely gorgeous as you.' He lowered his voice. 'You are very beautiful, you know that? Far too good for any demon. I'd love to know more about you when you've healed. I want to show you my palace – poets have described my gardens and fountains as the most picturesque in the world. Do you like horses?'

Her heart went cold. Another one.

'And that was exactly the wrong thing to say,' he said, amused. 'You've just escaped the clutches of a demon and now here I am, trying to ...'

'Own me,' she said.

'I don't own any of my wives,' he said. 'It's more like they own me.'

She looked pointedly at him.

'Wah,' he said, still amused. 'It's been a while since I've failed so comprehensively to charm a woman. Were you pretending to be interested in men and the bracelet forced you to love him?' The Tiger changed to a tall, muscular, platinum-haired woman. 'Because I do female just as well.'

She stiffened and went even colder.

'Argh,' the Tiger said, and changed back to male. He put his head in his hands. 'I concede. You win. I give up.' He looked into her eyes, full of genuine kindness. 'If there's anything you need, just tell the staff here. If you want to talk to me again – about your family, about what you're doing with your life, about how I can help you – just ask for me. I'll be here.' He rose. 'I should ask Emma for advice about how to handle you.' He smiled down at her. 'I'd really like to see more of you. But only if it's what you wish.'

He went out and she relaxed back onto her pillow. She allowed herself a small sigh of longing – he was the most powerfully attractive man she'd ever seen and his sympathy was heartbreaking. His fury would probably be just as destructive if he ever found out what she was.

7

Fion tapped on the door. 'Can I come in?'

'Sure.' Mei put the romance novel to one side. 'Uh, this is the last one. Do you have any more?'

'The Tiger has more than a hundred wives. We have *thousands* of them.'

Mei chuckled.

'I don't need to give you any more books,' Fion said. 'The results of this morning's X-rays came back and your legs are fine. The doctor will be in later to take the plaster off, and we'll take you home.'

Mei took Fion's hand and squeezed it. 'Thank you!'

'The Tiger asked me to pass a message on. That you can stay if you like, and get to know him. He'd like to get to know you.'

'You're asking me to date your own husband?' Mei said, incredulous.

'I know,' Fion said. 'It sounds ridiculous. But where the Tiger is concerned, we're all friends together, and we share the joy of being with him.' She patted Mei's hand. 'Being with him is a hundred times better than being with an ordinary man, and I can't imagine how it would compare to being with a cruel demon. He is the kindest and most generous husband a woman could ask for.'

'It's really that good?'

'It's wonderful,' Fion said. 'We are queens in this heavenly palace. He gives us anything we desire, and the most wonderful thing he gives us is himself.'

'To share,' Mei said.

Fion shrugged. 'He's usually too much for one woman to handle by herself.'

Mei stared at Fion.

'I mean it,' Fion said.

Mei giggled.

'So will you talk to him?'

'No. I need to go home to my family.'

'At least think about it.'

'I will.'

'What are you hiding, Mei?' Fion became more serious. 'You've done six weeks' worth of healing in two. And I've never

seen a Chinese person with hair that bright red unless they were
–'

'I'm not a demon,' Mei said.

'The Tiger agrees with you. So what are you? A Shen? Descendent of a Shen fallen from Heaven?'

'No. I'm an ordinary human.'

'You can trust us, Mei. You aren't a demon and you claim not to be a Shen and we know for a fact that you're not an ordinary human ... so what are you?'

'I can have the plaster off? I can go home?'

'Answer the question, Mei.'

'You won't take the plaster off unless I tell you?'

Fion tilted her head and looked pointedly at Mei.

'Can we just say my grandmother was a nature spirit – neither Shen nor demon, just a part of the natural world – and leave it at that? I don't even know what my grandmother was, she died before I was born. I didn't inherit anything special from her except for the hair and a slightly enhanced healing ability. Apart from that, I'm completely normal.'

Fion rose. 'I believe you. Let's take the plaster off and send you home.' She opened the door and turned back to smile at Mei. 'We've organised someone to go with you and make sure you're okay.'

After Fion had gone out, Mei thumped the bed next to her with frustration. All she needed, a nanny tagging along with her to watch her every move.

The doctor came in later that day with the X-rays and a tray of instruments. His head was still that of a lion's, but Mei had become accustomed to it and even managed to understand the expressions in his lion face.

He studied Mei, his light brown eyes crinkling up at the corners with merriment. 'Two weeks. Your left leg was broken in three places, and now it's like it never happened. Are you sure you aren't one of us?'

'I'm not a Shen,' she said.

'You're sure as hell something special,' the doctor said, almost to himself, as he put the tray of instruments to one side. He pulled out a large pair of scissors. 'Let's see if we can just cut it off without using the power saw.'

Mei sat rigid and untrusting on the bed as the points of the scissors approached her crotch. She was intensely aware of her nakedness under the short hospital gown, but the doctor was wearing a wedding band and made no attempt to touch her inappropriately. He took a great deal of care as he cut, and as he reached her inner thigh he slowed to make sure that he didn't injure her, at the same time ensuring she stayed covered by the gown. When he'd cut through the entire cast he lifted it away from her leg and brushed the plaster off. The skin of her leg smelled flat and stale after two weeks without washing, and she wondered how pungent it was for the half-Shen.

She wanted to scratch her leg so badly that she grabbed the sheets and held them.

'Let me get the other one off, then you can go take a shower,' the doctor said.

A short round young man came in, saw what was happening, turned around and went out.

'It's okay, Smallcat, I'm nearly done,' the doctor said.

'Tell me when she's decent and I'll come back in,' Smallcat said.

'Smallcat?' Mei said, amused.

'It's his nickname,' the doctor said. 'Very unusual for the son of the White Tiger to be a small forest cat. You should see him,' he stopped cutting and smiled at her, a disconcerting expression on his lion face. 'He's not much bigger than a housecat.' He returned to cutting the plaster. 'Dad doesn't know what to do with him.'

'Oh no,' Mei said, realising why Smallcat was there.

'What?' the doctor said, stopping. 'Did I hurt you?'

'He's my nanny,' Mei said with dismay. 'He's going to take me home and look after me.'

The doctor chuckled, a rasping sound in his lion throat. 'He's a lucky man.' He finished the plaster. 'There you go, have a shower and clean up, Lady Fion's put some clothes for you in the closet.'

'Thank you,' Mei said.

The room was empty when she came out of the shower in the clothes Fion had given her, tottering on her newly released legs. She walked up and down a few times, exercising her atrophied muscles. She stopped at the window, and for the first time saw more than just the sky.

The hospital building was on the side of a hill, and terraced red-stone building with arched doors and windows spread over the hillside below her. People wandered the breezeways and sat next to fountains in gardens rich with greenery. A brilliantly red bird, with wings and tail of purple and blue peacock-like feathers, flew down and landed next to a woman working on a laptop as she sat on the grass under a tree. The bird's head was level with the woman's as she sat, and she greeted it with a smile. The phoenix changed to an Indian woman wearing a red sari embroidered with peacock feathers that matched her own plumage. She embraced the sitting woman, and they sat together, holding hands to study the computer and discuss its contents.

Mei wondered where her nanny was. She went to the door and opened it, to find him lying in cat form next to the corridor wall. He was about twice as big as an ordinary housecat, pale silvery grey with large black spots and a cute white face with twitching whiskers. He changed to human and jumped to his feet. 'Sorry.'

'Are you the one taking me home?' she said.

He nodded.

'Okay. Let me put my stuff together.'

'Can I come in?'

She shrugged. 'Sure.'

He entered; he was about the same age as her, but half a head shorter and overweight, with his stomach bulging over the top of his jeans. They'd brought her handbag from the demon house, but not her luggage; at least she had her wallet and identity documents.

'You can take me home?' she said.

'I can. Tell me where you live and I'll drop you right there. I haven't inherited much power from my father, I'm very small, but I can teleport.'

'And then you'll come straight back here, right? I don't need more than that.' She bowed slightly. 'Tell your father thank you on my behalf, and Fion as well. I sincerely appreciate their kindness in my hour of need.'

And no thanks for killing my husband before I had that damn piece of paper, she added to herself.

'Dad's ordered me to stay with you for a week or so and make sure you're all right,' Smallcat said. 'I have access to his financial assets and we'll see what we can do about compensating you for what you've lost.' His gaze was judgemental. 'But I can't see why he should, it was all wealth gained from demonic activity. You should be left with nothing.'

'Tony paid me better than average for a female accountant, but even then it wasn't enough to support my family,' she said. 'My brother's profoundly disabled and caring for him is a full-time job for both my parents.'

'I'm sure a human boss would have paid you just as well,' he said. 'If you work with demons you deserve everything you get.'

She opened her mouth, then changed her mind about what she was going to say. She checked she had everything, and threw her bag over her shoulder. 'Can you take me home now?'

He held his hand out. 'Tell me where your home is and we're there.'

She gave him directions to the office building. Everything blanked out around them, there was a moment of complete silence, then the noise of traffic hit her and they were in front of the building. The doors were locked on the Sunday afternoon, so she swiped her electronic key to enter the empty lobby. She slammed the door behind her, but he shoved his foot in to stop it and followed her. She bolted to the lifts, used her security key to enable them, and continuously jabbed the lift button. The doors opened, she went inside, and he followed her.

'This doesn't look like a residential building,' he said as the doors closed.

'I'm home. I'm safe. You can go now,' she said without looking at him.

'I think I'll hang around.'

The lift bell dinged and the doors opened. She raced out with her ID in her hand, swiped the electronic lock next to the entrance door, ran through and closed it in his face.

She turned around and leaned on the door with relief; lost him.

He appeared in front of her. 'Yeah, that won't work.'

'I don't need you any more!' she said as she pushed past him towards her office.

'I want to see what you do,' he said, quietly amused. 'If we can find more demonic activity to shut down, Dad might actually be pleased with me for a change.'

She stopped and rounded on him. 'Looking for approval from your father, are you? Daddy issues?'

He didn't reply. Mei headed for her office – fortunately it was Sunday, and with the boss on 'sick leave' the place was deserted. She sat at her desk. Smallcat stood behind her as she booted up her computer and logged in.

'You know, technically you don't work here any more,' he said. 'In fact, nobody works here any more. It's only a matter of time before our reports of your boyfriend's – '

'Husband,' she snapped.

He continued. '… death reach the police here in Hong Kong, and as we killed everything in the Nest, there's no next of kin. The company will be shut down and the assets sold. The staff will receive a weeks' salary and the rest will go to the Government.'

'Look.' She spun in her chair to speak to him. 'This company – the legal side of it – employs two hundred and seventeen people. You probably don't understand small details like paying for food and rent, being a Prince of Heaven as you are … '

'They can find work somewhere else!'

'Yes they can,' she said. 'But they need an income while they do it. I know it'll all be shut down, but I'd like to delay it long enough to give them the best head start that I can. If this company is shut down right now, they'll be out on the streets with no income and bills to pay.'

He blinked at her.

She turned back and picked up the phone to call home.

'Wei?'

'It's me.'

'Mei! Where were you? What – '

'Listen, Ma Ma.'

'—happened, we only received – '

'Ma Ma, stop and listen, *there's a Shen here.*'

Her mother went silent.

'Some Celestials raided the Nest in Swatow just as we were having the wedding ceremony. They killed all of them. Tony's dead. The Shen injured me in the fight, but they looked after me and brought me back home today. One of them is here with me right now.'

'I understand,' her mother said. 'Where are you?'

'At the office, doing the obvious. When I'm done here, I'll go *back to Tony's apartment* and come see you in a couple of days. I just wanted to tell you that *everything's fine*, and *I'm safe now*.'

'She's at the office?' Ba Ba said in the background. 'Is Tony there?'

'They owe you compensation for injuring you,' Ma Ma said.

Mei eyed Smallcat. 'They seem to think that since the income was demon-related, I'm not owed anything.'

'What about the rest of Tony's staff?' Ma Ma said. 'They can't just fire them!'

'I'll arrange good severance pay for everybody, and come visit you as soon as it's done. It will probably take a couple of days, so I'll stay in the *apartment I share with Tony* until it's all fixed and the Shen's gone home.'

'I understand, Mei, but don't put yourself at risk to help them. Sometimes I think you care too much.'

'I don't think anyone can care too much. I'll see you soon, okay? Give Ba Ba and Di Di a big hug for me.'

'I will.'

'Hey! I want to talk to her!' Ba Ba said in the background, but Ma Ma hung up. A couple of minutes later the phone rang and Mei pulled the plug out.

'Can you run the company yourself long enough to take care of the staff?' Smallcat said.

'I'll give it a damn good try,' she said. 'He promoted me to CEO a month ago, I have the seniority to wrap things up, I just need to keep the company going for a few more days.' She ran her hand over her red ponytail with exasperation. 'If your damn father had waited one more day to kill him, I would have been his legal wife and inherited everything.' She spun in her chair towards him. 'Can you tell the government that he's brain-damaged or something and that I'm his legal guardian with power of attorney?'

'Celestials don't lie,' he said with forced dignity. 'Now that you're home and safe we'll notify the authorities that he died in China.'

'Can't you delay it?'

His expression softened. 'I have no control over it. Dad's legal team will take over.'

She had a brilliant idea. 'I saw you in cat form. Can you shapeshift?'

'Into what?'

She used her token to enter the accounting system, then Tony's master password to open the human resources database. She scrolled with dismay through the staff records. Yee Teng was paying for her father's chemotherapy, and KP Poon's wife had just had twins. 'Into Tony, stupid! If you can take his form and hold things together for a few days, I can give them a really good bonus and excellent reference letters, and send them on their way.'

'Oh,' he said, and dropped his voice. 'No. Cat or this human form. I'm very...' His voice trailed off and he sniffed the air. 'Do you smell that?'

She sniffed the air as well; burnt rubber and sewage. Demon. 'I thought you killed them all!' She quickly closed the HR database with a mix of delight and dismay at the thought of Tony being alive. 'It could be Tony.' She sniffed the air again. 'No, it doesn't quite –'

The outer office door slammed with a huge crash, followed by the sound of glass shattering, and she jumped to her feet and turned to see. It was Tony's mother, in her red silk dress, storming down the hall towards them.

Smallcat's voice was high-pitched with terror. 'A Mother.'

'Damn straight, little Shen,' Tony's mother said. She stopped in the doorway. 'Are you all right, my darling Mei?'

Mei took a step forward and dropped to one knee. 'Mother. I am so glad you're alive.' She reached back blindly with her left hand to touch Smallcat's ankle, and couldn't find it.

'Is this little Shen hurting you, dear?' Tony's mother said.

'I've been trying to lose him, but he can *teleport*,' Mei said with heavy meaning, still trying to find Smallcat's ankle. She patted the carpet behind her.

'Good girl, he looks delicious,' Tony's mother said. 'Once I've eaten him, do you mind helping me access the computer system? I want to see how much money my son had locked away here. You can help me.'

'Of course I will. But be careful, Mother, he can teleport,' Mei said, finding his foot and getting a firm grip on it. She squeezed it hard. '*Now.*'

'Oh,' Smallcat said. The office disappeared around them.

They landed in the middle of Kowloon Park. Mei staggered to her feet, dizzy with relief, then collapsed to sit on a park bench and put her face in her hands.

'She *is* your mother!' Smallcat said.

'She's Tony's mother, didn't you hear her?' Mei said. She glared up at Smallcat. 'Are you completely stupid? She was about to eat you, then force me to transfer the company's assets to her before she ate me as well.'

'I see.' He flopped to sit on the park bench next to her. 'So what do we do? She might eat the staff when they go in tomorrow morning.'

'Oh, she'll definitely eat them, human flesh is a delicacy for them and she hasn't eaten one in ages,' Mei said. 'The two of us together aren't big enough to destroy her, though.' She turned to look into his guileless face. 'I can get help, but you have to promise not to tell anyone who it is.'

Smallcat was talking at the same time. 'I can ask my father, he can take down a big Mother like that easily.' His expression went strange as he heard what she'd said. 'Tell anyone who who is?'

'Never mind, a Shen as big as your father will have no problem,' Mei said. 'Once she's gone we can sort the company out and fold it up.' She held her hand out. 'Will you help me?'

'There won't be anything to fold up, she's in the computer system taking all the assets.'

'No she isn't.' Mei raised her key ring, holding the token that generated the random access passcode. 'She doesn't have access to the financials without this.'

He hesitated for a moment, then shook her hand. 'All right.'

'Thank you.' She released his hand and waited.

He sat looking at her.

'Father, talking, yes?' she said.

'Oh,' he said, pulled a mobile phone out of his pocket, and pressed a single button.

'One,' the man on the other end said, clearly audible to Mei.

'Michael, it's Silvercat. Dad sent me down with this woman from the Swatow raid – '

'You're in the field? You're not trained for that!'

'It was supposed to be a risk free housekeeping mission,' Smallcat said. 'You remember that raid in Swatow? I was ordered to take Twenty-five's human wife home, and it's all gone to hell.'

'How to hell?'

'Twenty-five's Mother is still alive, and it came after the human wife.'

'Is she okay?'

'Yes, but the Mother's in the company offices raiding the assets and it'll probably eat the staff when they turn up tomorrow morning. I think we may need Dad to take it out.'

'Fuck,' Michael said on the other end. 'Hold on, I'll see where he is.'

'You've been around Dad too much,' Smallcat said.

'Thanks a lot.' He was silent for a moment. 'He's on his way, he actually sounded pleased to be dragged out of Court. Where are you?'

Smallcat looked around. 'Um, a park with high-rises all around it, and some truly awful sculptures on a long walkway, sort of like a piazza – '

'Kowloon Park Sculpture Walk,' Mei said loudly.

'Is that the wife?' Michael said.

'Yeah,' Smallcat said.

'Is she as hot as they say she is?'

Mei stared, challenging, at Smallcat while he studied her.

He shrugged. 'I suppose.'

She tossed her head and pulled some strands of hair from the long ponytail to frame her face.

'He's on his way,' Michael said. 'He'll contact you telepathically when he lands.'

Smallcat winced. 'He'll have to call me, I'm not telepathic. I can't talk back.'

'Oh yeah. Just a sec … Okay I told him. He'll be there in five.'

Smallcat pressed the phone button and turned to study Mei. 'Is that hair for real?'

'One hundred per cent natural,' Mei said, not sure whether his casual disinterest was worse than the usual drooling intensity she received.

'So you're part-demon?'

'I'm an ordinary human!'

'The fact that you know there's an alternative to "ordinary human" proves that you aren't one,' he said.

Mei pointedly ignored him and turned to watch the people, who were wandering around looking at the sculptures. Her phone rang in her bag and she pulled it out. 'Wei?'

It was her mother. 'Mei, are you still at the office?'

'No, Tony's mother showed up. She wants the company assets; she must have been waiting for me. I had to run. Don't go near there.'

There was a long silence.

'Ma Ma?'

Ma Ma's voice was choked with tears. 'He missed you so much, he was so worried, he is such a softie. He had to see you to make sure you were okay. I couldn't talk him out of it, so I'm minding Di Di … '

Mei shot to her feet. 'Ba Ba went there?'

The only response was a single sob on the other end of the line.

Smallcat's phone rang and he answered it. 'Small … Silvercat.'

'So where are you?' the White Tiger said on Smallcat's phone.

'Ma Ma,' Mei said. 'We have help coming. Call him, tell him to stay away from the office. Okay? Call him now, and tell him to stay away.'

'East side of the round amphitheatre with the really ugly bronze in the middle,' Smallcat said, standing as well to look around.

'Okay,' Ma Ma said.

'I'm coming,' the Tiger said. His footsteps were audible, along with the clink of metal. 'Okay I see you.' He hung up.

He appeared striding towards them and Mei quailed. This wasn't the kind gentleman who had been so sympathetic in the hospital; this White Tiger was all warrior in white and gold armour and a sword at his side.

'Hi Dad,' Smallcat said, obviously intimidated.

'Michael told me all about it. So where's this big Mother?'

Smallcat pointed. 'Office building two blocks over, tenth floor.'

'All right, leave it to me,' the Tiger said, and moved to leave. He stopped when Mei's phone rang again.

It was her mother. 'Is the Shen still there?'

'Yes,' Mei said. 'Two of them now, one's going to take the Mother down.'

'Tell them they don't need to, we've come to an arrangement. She'll swap your father for me. She doesn't want him, she wants me. Apparently I will taste better.'

'What? No!' Mei said, horrified, and the Shen shared a look.

'Ditch the Shen,' Ma Ma said. 'Go to the lobby of the building, and wait there. I'll leave Di Di for you to mind when I go up, and you can collect your father when he comes down.'

'She'll eat both of you!' Mei wailed.

'Then we'll die together,' Ma Ma said. 'I don't want to live without him, dear Mei. I'm sorry.'

'The White Tiger Shen is here,' Mei said. 'He can do it. He can save him.'

'No, Mei! Get rid of him. Don't let the White Tiger anywhere near us.'

The Tiger was waving his hand in front of Mei's face, and with a soft sound of frustration he grabbed the phone. 'Listen to me. I'm one of the most powerful demon destroyers around, and I can take this thing down. I can shapeshift as well, so meet us in the lobby, and I'll take your form and go up as you. Even if it does try to eat your husband, I can destroy it and save him.'

Ma Ma was silent for a long time.

'Are you there?' the Tiger said.

'Promise me one thing,' Ma Ma said.

'I will do my best to save him, I won't let him be "collateral damage",' the Tiger said. 'You have my word.'

'No,' Ma Ma said. 'Promise me that you won't hurt either me or my son.'

Smallcat and the Tiger shared a look.

'What are you?' the Tiger said.

'Humans will die if you don't destroy that demon, and to destroy it you need us,' Ma Ma said. 'Your word that you won't harm any of us!'

'Do I have a reason to hurt you?' the Tiger said.

'Promise!' Ma Ma said, desperate. 'I'm nearly at the building, we don't have much time! She'll know I'm close!'

'I won't harm you or your son. I'm only here to take out the demon.'

'All right, we're waiting for you,' Ma Ma said. She lowered her voice. 'I am so sorry, Mei.' She hung up and the Tiger handed the phone back to Mei.

'Why is she apologising to you?' Smallcat said.

'We don't have time for this, we need to be at the building now,' Mei said, and put her hand on Smallcat's shoulder.

'Show me where,' the Tiger said, and put his hand on Smallcat's shoulder as well.

The park disappeared around them, and again there was a moment of complete silence before the wind and traffic noises reappeared. They were outside the empty office building, and Ma Ma was standing inside, next to Di Di in his wheelchair. The Tiger walked straight through the glass lobby wall, then drew his sword and approached Ma Ma menacingly. Mei used her key to open the door and she and Smallcat entered the lobby as well, the empty space echoing around them. Smallcat moved to the side of the lobby, his whole attitude now one of alert defence.

'You vowed not to hurt them!' Mei said.

The Tiger stopped next to the wheelchair. Di Di made some garbled sounds of delight and tried to grab him with his twisted hands.

'Hong Lai. Long time no see. You owe me thirty-four thousand yuan and three thoroughbred horses,' the Tiger said to Ma Ma, his voice like gravel.

Mei's mouth flopped open.

Ma Ma changed to fox form – slightly larger than a natural fox with three full tails – and huddled quivering in front of the lifts. She wrapped her tails around her and hid her face in them.

The Tiger strode to the lift and grabbed Ma Ma by the scruff of her neck. He raised her to eye level and she sagged in his hand, her little white-tipped paws dangling.

'That's from 1921,' he said, 'so with interest the debt is probably thirty-four *million* now. Isn't there a death sentence hanging over you from the last time you ripped someone off?'

Ma Ma straightened in the Tiger's hand and looked him in the eye. 'If you hadn't killed my daughter's husband I could have paid you back!'

The Tiger shook Ma Ma so hard that Mei thought he would break her neck, and she made high-pitched yelps of pain.

'Her husband? Her *husband*? You married your own daughter off to a fucking *demon*!' he roared. 'What sort of mother are you?'

'Stop it!' Mei shouted, pulling at the Tiger's arm. 'It was my idea.'

He scowled at her. 'The hell it was.'

'All my idea!' Mei said. 'He really was in love with me.'

'Demons only love one person in the world, and that's themselves,' the Tiger said. 'He gave you that bracelet to make you love him, the controlling asshole.'

Ma Ma straightened in his grasp and turned her small black nose towards Mei. 'He gave you a cursed bracelet?'

'That was beside the point, marrying him would free the family. It was worth it,' Mei said.

'No, it wasn't, Mei,' Ma Ma said from where she hung from the Tiger's grasp, her voice sounding strange coming from the fox's mouth. 'And I wouldn't let you do it again. It was a huge mistake.'

'I would do it again in a second,' Mei said, defiant.

'And I would stop you,' Ma Ma said. Her voice became desperate. 'We don't have time for this, my husband is human

98

and that Snake Mother has him. Let me go, let me trade myself for him.'

'You married a human?' the Tiger said.

'I went straight,' Ma Ma said. 'I've been living as a human physician for thirty years.' Her voice rose in pitch. 'I have two children!'

'This is your son?'

'He's cursed. He has the mind of a child,' Ma Ma said.

'Leave them alone! You promised!' Mei said.

The Tiger relaxed but remained alert. 'Is her father really up there?'

Ma Ma sagged in his grasp. 'He really is. Please, save him, he may only be a human but he's my whole world.'

'You gave your word, Tiger,' Mei said.

'That I did,' the Tiger said. He lowered Ma Ma and she retook human form. 'Let's rescue this human. You,' he glared at Ma Ma, 'I will deal with later.'

'When this is over, you can have me,' Ma Ma said. 'You can do what you like to me. Just don't hurt any of them, my son is harmless and my husband and daughter are *human*!'

Smallcat came to them, putting his phone away. 'Are we good to do this?'

The Tiger changed to the image of Ma Ma and nodded. 'Wait outside. I'll contact you telepathically when it's safe to come up.'

The lift doors opened. A monster held Ba Ba in front of it with a knife to his throat. The scent hit Mei and she realized that it was Tony's mother, in demon form. Her front half looked human, but without skin, and her back end was a snake. Her skinless head nearly touched the ceiling of the lift as she balanced on her snake coils. Ba Ba was rigidly standing on his toes because of her height, and his eyes rolled with terror.

Everybody took a step back, and Mei grabbed Di Di's wheelchair and raced to the external doors to take him out where he'd be safe. The doors clicked in front of her; locked by the demon.

'I said I'd swap the human for the fox,' Tony's mother said. 'But which one is the fox?'

Both Ma Mas stepped forward. 'I am.'

'I can't tell which of you is the real fox,' the demon said. 'Never mind, I'll take the girl. She's my daughter now, isn't she? She has to obey me. She can strip my son's company for me.'

'Mei run!' Ba Ba said.

Tony's mother yanked her arm up under Ba Ba's chin and he flopped, unconscious.

'I'll come with you,' Mei said. 'Let him go.'

The demon gestured with her head for Mei to approach.

Mei released the handles of Di Di's wheelchair and eased herself carefully towards the lift with her hands up and visible.

The Tiger made soft sound of frustration. Ba Ba was an effective shield.

'Press the lift button,' the demon said.

Mei pressed the lift button and the doors opened behind the demon. The demon backed into the lift and put her snake tail in the door to stop it from closing.

'In,' the demon said.

'Let him go,' Mei said.

'I'll leave him in the lift.'

Mei joined them in the lift, turned to see her desperate mother's face, and the doors closed on them. She was alone in the lift with the huge demon. The small space was rank with the foul smell. For a moment Mei thought her father wasn't breathing, then saw his chest move. He was okay, just unconscious.

'Hurt my father and I won't help you,' Mei said.

'You'll help me or I'll eat you,' the demon said.

'You're going to eat me anyway. Let my father go and I'll do the finance thing for you.'

'Humph. Whatever.' The demon dropped Ba Ba and he crumpled, hitting the back of his head on the lift wall on the way down. Mei carefully lifted him so he was sitting against the wall of the lift, then kissed him good bye on his forehead. He was still breathing, so she hoped the damage wasn't too bad. The Shen would help him when she was gone.

The doors opened. The demon grabbed Mei's wrist and dragged her through the cubicles – Mei's own original cubicle, where all of this had started – to her office. She threw Mei into her office chair and loomed over her. 'Get me all Twenty-five's money.'

Mei turned in her chair to face the computer and restarted it. 'I need your bank account details to put the money in.'

'Phone,' the demon said.

Mei pointed at the office phone. The demon picked up the handset, then shook it. 'No dial tone?'

'Oh.' Mei plugged the phone back in and pressed the button to restart it.

As the demon pressed the buttons, Mei opened the accounting system, her shaking hands making it clumsy and difficult.

'Any chance of me having a job with your company?' Mei said with terrified enthusiasm. 'I'm a good accountant.'

'I'm going to hide for twenty years, the Tiger will be after me. I won't need any staff where I'm going.'

'You could always let me go,' Mei said, the false keenness making her voice brittle.

The demon put her hand on Mei's shoulder and Mei jumped. She spoke with genuine kindness. 'Ah, dear Mei. I would love to, I really would, but you'll know my banking details and you're far too clever to trust with that sort of information.'

'What if I promise not to do anything with it?'

The demon squeezed her shoulder and released it. 'The word of a fox? Really, child.'

'Then at least make it quick,' Mei said, her voice quivering as much as her hands were.

'You won't feel a thing, Little Red. I promise.' She barked into the phone. 'About time you answered. I need my bank account details, all of them, for transferring money in.' She listened for a moment. 'You have two minutes. Hurry!'

Mei pushed a pen and paper to the demon as she opened the bank accounts. 'The company has fifteen different bank accounts for the separate aspect of the bus—'

'I don't care what is where, I want it all. Now,' the demon said. She turned to speak into the phone. 'Where are the bank details? Hurry up!'

'What about the accounts that require twenty-four hours' notice before they're withdrawn?' Mei said, suddenly full of hope. 'You'll have to wait to get that money. I can do it for you tomorrow.'

'How much?'

'Thirty million US,' Mei said.

'And how much is the total amount?'

'Forty. You'll lose more than half of it if you aren't prepared to wait,' Mei said, the fierce hope even stronger. 'Just one day and you can have all forty million rather than just ten.'

'Hmm.' The demon pulled the pen and paper and wrote the bank account details as they were read to her over the phone. 'Zero. Four. Zero. Four. Four. Four.'

Mei winced at the repetition of the unlucky four, the death number.

'Forty million. Ten million. Hmm.' She put the phone down. 'Is this just a delaying tactic so you can live longer, and give your little kitty friends a chance to rescue you?'

'Yes about the rescue, but I'm not lying about the money.'

'Here's the account details. Start transferring,' the demon said. 'Ten or forty. Thirty million dollars is a hell of a lot of money to pass up.'

Please let me live another day and give the Tiger a chance to save me, Mei thought desperately at her.

'Nah,' the demon said. 'Not worth it. Transfer the ten million. And I'm watching you, so don't mess around trying to make it last longer. If it isn't done in ten minutes I'll eat you anyway.'

Mei couldn't control the tiny sob that escaped her, turned to face the computer and pulled a tissue out to wipe her eyes. She wanted to be brave, face death and look it in the eye, but she didn't feel brave; she wanted to cry for a week. She wished she'd never met Tony, and wanted more than anything to be back in her tiny bunk bed in that wonderful rat-infested apartment with her family.

She pressed the button on the security token to bring up the confirmation number so she could start the transfers. It took her five minutes to consolidate the accounts ready for the transfer, but busying herself with the numbers helped to keep her mind off the monster hanging over her shoulder. She saw something in the corner of her eye, and turned to see. Smallcat – a dark grey blur in feline form – shot across the office and latched onto the demon's tail.

The demon slithered in circles, trying to dislodge him. 'Get off me!' She reached down to pull him off but he had his paws around her tail with a good grip. Another big cat loped down the hall, its paws thudding on the carpet, and jumped onto the demon's shoulders, across the back of her neck. It was an enormous white tiger, bigger than a lion. Mei leaped out of her office chair and ran to the side of the room at the sight of it. She couldn't understand how the demon could carry the weight of both cats. Tony's mother pulled at the tiger, but it sunk its teeth into the back of her neck, its claws into her shoulders, and held her.

The demon spun in circles, crashing into the walls, but the tiger couldn't be dislodged. Smallcat growled as he worried the demon's snake tail.

The demon spun again, its skinless face a mass of rage and pain, and when it was facing the office door, an arrow sung through the air and into its shoulder.

Mei turned to see through the door; it was Ma Ma. Petite, slim, middle-aged Ma Ma was aiming a crossbow at the demon.

'Out of the way, Mei!' she shouted.

'The eyes, Lai, the eyes!' the Tiger shouted through a mouthful of demon.

Mei jumped back as another arrow shot past the demon's head and buried itself into the wall. The demon spun again, trying to prise the Tiger from her shoulders.

'For fuck's sake hit it in the goddamn *eyes*, woman!' the Tiger shouted.

Another arrow hit the demon on the chest and stuck there, and it screamed.

'No, in the –' the Tiger began, but Mei had had enough. She ran to the demon, leapt to grab its shoulder, ripped the arrow out of its chest and thrust it into the demon's eye. She jumped as far as she could from its grasping hands. The two cats threw themselves gracefully away as the demon exploded into black goo, then landed on the floor and changed to human form.

Smallcat approached Mei. 'Are you all right?'

'Ma Ma!' Mei shouted, and ran to hug her.

Ma Ma dropped the crossbow and embraced Mei. 'Did it hurt you?'

'No. I'm fine.' Mei sagged in her mother's grasp and it all came out. The tears that had been bottled up while the demon had been standing over her were released in a gush of fear and relief. Someone handed her a tissue and she mopped her eyes.

Smallcat put his hand on her shoulder. 'You're safe now. It's gone.'

'Thank you,' she choked into the tissue.

Ma Ma squeezed her shoulder. 'Mei, I know you've had a terrible fright but you must pull yourself together, because your father's hurt and we need to take him to a hospital.'

'She's had far too much nastiness happen to her in the last few weeks, it's not surprising she's lost it,' the Tiger said kindly.

The news about her father was like a bucket of cold water over Mei and she straightened. 'I'm okay. I'm sorry.' She took some huge deep gasping breaths and went to her desk to find more tissues. She grabbed a few and mopped at her face again. 'Do we need to call an ambulance?'

'Our medical centre is at your disposal,' the Tiger said. 'He will heal three times faster in the Western Palace.'

'No,' Mei said.

'They're right, Mei, he'll heal faster there, but I can't go,' Ma Ma said.

'You are welcome, Madam Lee,' the Tiger said. 'I will protect you, your family need you.'

Ma Ma put her arm around Mei's shoulder. 'I'll stay and mind Di Di. You go with your father and look after him.'

'We'll protect you, Mrs Lee. You will be safe in the Western Palace,' the Tiger said.

'A fox among all you cats?' Ma Ma said. She shook her head. 'Please, take them and care for them. If you can uncurse my son I will be indebted to you forever. But I know I'm not welcome in the Heavens, you said yourself that I have a death sentence hanging over me. I will wait here.'

'I can rescind it, I have the authority,' he said.

They went to the lift; Ba Ba was still slumped against the back wall, his eyes open and glazed. Mei crouched to speak to him and put her hand on his cheek. 'Are you okay, Ba Ba?'

Ba Ba mumbled something incoherent and grabbed her arm as the doors closed.

The Tiger picked Ba Ba up like a child, cradling him in his arms, and the lift went down. Di Di was waiting for them in the lift lobby, still with an uncomprehending grin on his face.

'This man needs a hospital right away,' the Tiger said. He put his hand on Ma Ma's shoulder. 'Take the kid.'

Smallcat put one hand on the wheelchair and everybody disappeared.

Mei was left alone in the building's lobby. She stood for a moment, stunned, with the fading Sunday afternoon light falling through the lobby windows and shining on the floor tiles around her. She tried the external doors; still locked. She went to the lift and pressed the button so she could return to the office and find her electronic key to open them.

The empty building echoed around her as she rode the lift up to the deserted offices. She sniffed the air regularly, but there was no trace of any demons. The office doors were broken and hanging open where Tony's mother had crashed through them. She went to her own executive office and looked out over the streets below, busy with Sunday evening crowds. It had been good while it lasted, spending a few short weeks as an executive with some real rewarding responsibility. She knew the Tiger's people wouldn't hurt her family, but she wondered how long it would be before she could see them again. And if the Tiger really could restore Di Di. And Ba Ba, poor Ba Ba. She leaned her forehead on the glass. She'd done it all to free her family and they'd ended up worse than when they started. No tears came; she was cried out. She sighed and went to her desk, logged back in, and cancelled the pending money transfer.

Tomorrow she would do the right thing by the staff, by giving them severance cheques and sending them on their way. But if she extracted money for herself, or tried to strip the firm's assets, the watching authorities would be aware of it and she could be up on charges of theft or fraud. She had the demon woman's account information now and could probably work the transfer the other way, but once again any huge deposit into her private funds would attract attention with her husband so newly dead. Perhaps if she created some accounts under an acquired business name – if she had the time to fix it before the whole thing collapsed. She'd worry about it tomorrow; maybe she'd hear from the Tiger about her family as well. Right now she needed to go home, and she needed the electronic door key to exit the building. She looked around for her bag; it was under the desk with its contents scattered across the floor. She climbed under the desk and proceeded to pick everything up.

The texture of the air changed, and it filled with the musky scent of big cat. Feet appeared next to the window and Mei went very still and quiet.

'Are you okay?' the Tiger said. He bent to see her. 'What are you doing under there?'

She sighed with relief and continued to pick up her things. 'The demon knocked my bag onto the floor.'

'Oh.' He went down on all fours and helped her.

They quickly worked together, tossing everything back into her bag. Fortunately he left the tampons for her to pick up and she didn't have that particular embarrassment to deal with.

'Are my family okay? How are my father and brother?'

'Your father will be okay. We're looking for someone who has the skills to uncurse your brother. I came back to collect you after they were settled.' He handed her pen to her, and climbed out from under the desk.

She pulled herself out to join him.

He moved close to her and she felt his warmth. 'We're looking after them. They'll be fine.'

She fiddled with her bag without looking up at him. 'Can you take me to see them?'

He put his hand on her arm; so strong. 'I can.' He raised his hand as if he was going to lift her chin, then dropped his hand again. 'Look at me?'

She looked up into his tawny eyes and her heart melted again at the compassion within them.

'You sacrificed so much to protect your family,' he said. 'Haven't you ever wanted anything for yourself?'

'Having my family whole and safe is what I want for myself,' she said.

He moved closer so they were touching along the lengths of their bodies, and she couldn't help herself; she put her arms around him. She felt the hard muscle of his back beneath the white silk, and she ran her hands over it, feeling the curves beneath.

His gaze became even more intense as he put one arm around her to hold her, and the other hand on her cheek. 'You should want more for yourself. I can give you anything you wish for.' He dropped his face to hers and she closed her eyes.

'I thought you were trying to set me up with Silvercat?' she said before their mouths met.

He stopped, his mouth so close it brushed hers as he spoke. 'I don't think he's your type.'

She reached up slightly to close the gap. He pulled her tighter, deepening the kiss, and she lost herself in the pleasure of touching him. Her hands worked their way under the silk of his shirt to slide inside his pants and over his tight behind, then up to trace the smooth muscles of his back. He moaned into her mouth and thrust gently. Tony had never kissed her like this, he didn't like kissing, but he was thrusting against her and ...

She was alone, and she opened her eyes. The Tiger was standing on the other side of the office with his arms spread wide and a look of complete bewilderment on his face.

'Did I hurt you?' he said, dropping his hands.

She looked around. She'd jumped backwards at least two metres and couldn't remember doing it. 'What happened?'

'I've seen that before,' he said. He stepped forward and she backed away. He leaned one hip on the desk. 'You flashed back to being with that demon.'

She put her hand over her mouth, suddenly nauseous.

'You need time,' he said softly. He raised his hand towards her. 'Hold my hand, and I'll take you to your family.'

She shook her head, still with her hand over her mouth.

'Do you need the bathroom?' he said.

She nodded, turned, and ran. She didn't make it to the bathroom, she stopped and threw up into one of the office wastepaper baskets. She crouched and bent over it, retching stomach acid with tears flowing from her eyes, mortified that the Tiger was seeing her like this. Hardly anything came up; the last thing she'd eaten was breakfast at the Tiger's hospital.

He came to her and put his hand on her back, making her even more ashamed. 'It's okay. I know it's embarrassing, but you've been through so much that it's not surprising.' He passed her a wet tissue and she wiped her mouth, nodding her thanks, then tossed it into the now foul-smelling bin.

She remained crouching, taking deep breaths to ease the nausea. He pressed something into her hand and she looked; a single-wrapped mint. He was a mind-reader because that was exactly what she needed.

'Go and rinse your face in the bathroom,' he said. 'I'll wait for you.'

She bundled the plastic bag out of the wastepaper basket to dispose of it but he put his hand on her arm to stop her.

'Leave it,' he said. 'I'll look after it. You go and wash your face, it will make you feel better.'

She hesitated; she'd made this mess and she should clean it up.

'It's okay,' he said, so gentle it broke her heart. 'I'll handle it. Look after yourself. If there's anything you need, just say it, I'll hear you.'

She nodded without looking at him and headed to the bathrooms behind the lifts.

When she came out the wastepaper basket was gone and he was standing in the office holding her bag. He passed it to her. 'You need time, Mei. Once your family are settled, you should come to my palace for a while and take a break.' He saw her face and smiled. 'Not like that. I can see that you're not ready for a new relationship. But you really do need some time to heal and my palace is the perfect place.'

She shook her head. 'I've just spent two weeks healing. I have to look after the staff here. Then I need to find a new job to support my family.'

'I understand,' he said, and held his hand out.

As she took his hand she knew he did.

8

They arrived in the medical centre where Mei had been treated for her broken legs. Her father was in a hospital bed similar to her own, and her mother was fussing over him. Smallcat sat next to Di Di in his wheelchair on one side of the room.

'I feel fine,' Ba Ba said. 'Here's my Mei Mei.'

Mei went to him and hugged him. 'How are you feeling?'

He gingerly touched his throat and winced. 'I feel a bit weak, but I'm ready to go home, right Red?'

Ma Ma patted his arm. 'Yes. I'll look after you.'

The Tiger fell to one knee.

'Whoa,' Smallcat said softly.

'Allow me to compensate you for the damage done to your family, Ah Lai,' the Tiger said. 'We were the ones that hurt your daughter, and we didn't protect your husband. It's my role as a Shen of Heaven to protect all citizens – of both Heaven and Earth – from the demons, and I failed.'

'I already owe you money, Bai Hu. I don't want to owe you more, so let's call it even,' Ma Ma said. 'Just take us home, and … ' she bent to speak more closely to him, 'keep your paws off my daughter.'

'Tiger, is the necklace cursing my brother?' Mei said. 'Like the bracelet was cursing me?'

The Tiger turned to her. 'What necklace?'

'The necklace!' Ma Ma said. 'You're right. Tony gave us a talisman to put on him before they left for China.'

The Tiger went to Di Di and checked his neck. He lifted the necklace over Di Di's head, and Di Di slumped forward.

Di Di didn't move for a long time, and Mei had a jolt of shock. 'He's not breathing!'

The Tiger returned the necklace, but Di Di didn't start breathing.

'Ma Ma do something!' Mei shouted.

'Red!' Ba Ba shouted at the same time, throwing the covers off and trying to get out of bed, then failing and falling back, clutching his throat.

Ma Ma moved like lightning. She grabbed Di Di, pulled him down onto the floor, laid him on his back, and started CPR. She blew into his mouth, holding his nose, then felt for a pulse.

'Back up, Ah Lai,' the Tiger said.

'How are you so calm? He's dying!' Ma Ma leaned into Di Di's chest. 'Get a crash cart!' she shouted.

'Smallcat pull her off,' the Tiger said.

'No!' Ma Ma said. 'Mei go look for a crash cart.'

'Don't move, Mei.' Smallcat went to Ma Ma and pulled her away from Di Di. She fought him. 'He's not breathing!'

Smallcat held her near Ba Ba. 'Dad can fix it.'

'Hurry! He'll die if you –' Mei shouted.

'Quiet,' the Tiger said, and glowed brilliantly white. He fell to one knee next to Di Di, put his hand on Di Di's chest, and closed his eyes. The shimmering silvery field around him surged into Di Di, and Di Di spasmed as if he'd received an electric shock.

Di Di inhaled loudly and snapped open his eyes.

The Tiger stepped back. 'There.'

Ma Ma and Mei ran to Di Di, and helped him to sit up.

'What happened? Mei!' Di Di tried to stand, and collapsed into their arms. 'Stay away from your boss, he's a demon! He wants you!'

'Tony did this to you?' Mei said. 'He can't have, he was with me when it happened.'

'His demon thralls did it. He wanted control of you,' Di Di said. 'He had a creep of an actress ready to spin you a story about needing a lot of money to uncurse me. He set you up to be his slave!' He struggled to rise but his muscles obviously weren't working. 'Leave the company and stay away from him.'

'He's dead,' Mei said.

'Who killed him?'

'I did,' the Tiger said.

Di Di looked around. 'Why are we in a hospital? Wait. This is Heaven.' He struggled to rise again. 'How long have I been out?'

'More than a year, dear Leung,' Mei said, and helped him back into the wheelchair. 'It will take a while for you to have your legs back.'

'Lord Bai Hu,' Di Di said with wonder.

The Tiger nodded acknowledgement.

'A holy Shen of Heaven: wow, are we in trouble. Are you okay, Ma Ma?'

110

'I'm fine,' Ma Ma said. 'We had some excitement but it's over now and we can all go home.'

Mei wiped the tears of joy from her eyes. 'Everybody's okay.' She looked up at the Tiger. 'Thank you so much. Can you return his muscles?'

'No,' the Tiger said. 'All he needs now is time.' He nodded to Ma Ma. 'Stay in one of my guest villas for a couple of days and let them recover.'

'No, we should go,' Ma Ma said.

'Stay if he's willing to help you, Ma Ma,' Di Di said. 'You know we'll heal much faster in Heaven.'

Ma Ma sagged with defeat. 'All right.'

'You know so much about this stuff,' Mei said, tapping his shoulder, 'and never told me.'

'Ma Ma wanted you to have a normal life. But since we're here I suppose you should know everything,' Di Di said. His voice dropped with misery. 'Oh no. This is awful. I don't believe it. Tell me it's not true.'

'What's not true?' Mei said, concerned.

'I'm wearing a *diaper*.'

The next morning Mei went to the office with Smallcat, both of them in business suits. The door was still hanging open and staff were milling in the central cubicle area, confused. They gathered around her.

'KP, can you find someone to fix the door, please?' she said.

'How's Tony? How are you? What *happened*?' Daniel said, looking from Mei to Smallcat.

'Tony's still in hospital, he's very unwell. Head injuries,' Mei said. She lowered her voice. 'The business has to go into receivership. We're closing.'

There was a chorus of dismay.

'You can run it, Mei!' Sandy said.

'There's something you need to know,' Mei said, gesturing towards Smallcat.

'I'm Inspector Mao from the Independent Commission Against Corruption,' Smallcat said. 'Unfortunately we discovered that your boss, Tony Wong, was involved in illegal activities across the border, and was using this company to

111

launder the money. We appreciate that he's incapable of answering the charges while he's brain-damaged as he is – '

'Brain damage?' PK said with dismay.

'But the company will be passed to auditors and business will have to cease.'

The staff didn't seem terribly surprised at that, and some of them looked questioningly at Mei. She tried to appear innocent.

'Before we close it down, we will arrange for all of you to receive full and generous severance pay, and Miss Lee will provide you with references. ICAC understands and sympathises with your difficulties, and the Government will give you introductions to a number of local companies that would be glad to gain your skills.'

There was another chorus of dismay.

'Did you know this was going on, Mei?' Sandy said.

'We are confident that Miss Lee had no idea,' Smallcat said. 'All the activities of this part of RedGold were completely legal, it was just his business – RedDevil – across the border in China that wasn't. Miss Lee didn't have anything to do with it.' He raised one hand to quell their protests. 'We're confident that none of you had anything to do with it.' He gestured towards Mei's corner office. 'Miss Lee, I would appreciate your assistance.'

'Of course, Inspector,' Mei said. She raised her voice. 'Don't worry, guys, I'll look after you.'

'If this part of the business is legal, then why can't you leave it running?' Sandy said.

'Because the owner is a criminal, and the profits are crime-related,' Smallcat said. 'Everything has to be confiscated as the proceeds of criminal activity. Go and pack up your desks, people, and we'll speak to each of you in turn.'

The staff stood confused as Mei and Smallcat went to her office.

Smallcat closed the office door behind them.

'Sit, Mei, you're as white as a ghost,' Smallcat said. 'Open your human resources system, and let's get to work.'

'Are you *sure* this is all legal?' Mei said. 'We're stripping the company.'

'I have several brothers in senior positions in the government here,' Smallcat said. He took a laptop out of the bag he was carrying and opened it on her desk. 'They'll handle the legal side; all we have to do is transfer the money out and give everybody their letters.'

They spent the rest of the day working together, dividing up the remaining funds held by the company and allocating them to the staff, as well as writing glowing reference letters for everybody.

Sandy was the last one. She came into the office and sat on the other side of the desk from them.

'Here's your severance,' Smallcat said, passing the cheque to her.

'And your reference letter,' Mei said, passing the envelope over the table.

Sandy wiped her eyes. 'I don't believe this is happening. Nasty Kwok was so lucky, retiring just before all this happened. How will I live...' She saw the cheque. 'Two hundred thousand?' Her eyes went wide. '*American* dollars?' She glanced up at Mei and Smallcat. 'This can't be right.'

'We can reduce the figure if you want,' Smallcat said. 'But that's the amount everybody's receiving.'

Sandy jumped to her feet with enthusiasm. 'I don't know whether to rent a bigger apartment for my family, or go overseas.'

'Do both,' Mei said.

Sandy opened the envelope containing reference letter, her hands shaking. She unfolded it and quickly perused it, flipping through the pages. She grinned at Mei and Smallcat. 'Thank you!'

'Keep in touch, Sandy,' Mei said.

Sandy bustled around the desk and put her arm around Mei's shoulder. 'Absolutely. But I'm going to London to see my parents first – they've never seen their grandchildren!'

'Those companies I've listed there will be glad to employ you when you return,' Smallcat said.

'I cannot believe this,' Sandy said, and jiggled with delight. 'I have to go tell my husband!' She ran out the door.

'She's the last one,' Mei said, studying the list. She nodded to herself; all done.

'Not the last,' Smallcat said, typing on his laptop. 'How much was your apartment in Diamond Hill worth?'

'About six million,' Mei said absently as she double-checked the figures.

'Done,' Smallcat said triumphantly, tapping the enter key. He took a cheque out of the printer. 'Yours.'

She took the cheque, then leaned back and stared at the number with shock.

'Your face is the same is Mrs Zhou's,' Smallcat said.

'I meant six million Hong Kong dollars. That's enough to buy *five* apartments,' Mei said. She double-checked the bank accounts; there was nothing left in the company. She turned to Smallcat and kissed him on the cheek, making him blush. 'Thank you. I completely forgot about myself when I worked the numbers out.'

'I know you did,' he said. He closed the computer and rose. 'Come on, I'll take you back to the Western Palace and you can have dinner with your family.'

Back at the Tiger's palace, Ma Ma, Ba Ba and Di Di were sitting on the terrace outside their guest villa, watching the Tiger's soldiers riding horses across the red sandy plain below the palace. Crinkled red mountains, so high the disappeared into the sky, rose from the other side of the plain – the fabled Kunlun Mountains of the West, where the most ancient of the deities lived. The air of the Heavens was purer and cleaner than any Mei had breathed before, a contrast that was even more obvious when she'd just come from the pollution of Hong Kong.

A pair of dragons flew overhead, glittering green in the setting sun, and a red phoenix, its feathers burning, followed them. The dragons saw the phoenix and they swooped and turned in the sky overhead, playing in the air. One of the riders on the plain below jumped off her horse, changed to a snow leopard, and leapt into the sky to join them, the four of them calling friendly jibes as they chased each other.

Mei sat with her family, who were rapt in the show above them. 'How is everybody?'

'We can go home tomorrow,' Ma Ma said. 'The Tiger's servants are making dinner for us, we don't have to do a thing.'

114

'The Shen are being so kind to us. I don't believe it,' Mei said.

'It's their nature,' Di Di said.

'Smallcat gave us six million dollars out of Tony's business.'

'That's enough to buy a new apartment!' Ba Ba said.

'Uh, six million *US*.'

'Oh.' Ma Ma sighed. 'That's so generous. Are you sure it's all legal?'

'I double-checked. It's all legal.' Mei cocked her head. 'Where did the crossbow come from?'

Ma Ma held her hand out and the crossbow appeared in it. She handed it to Mei. 'Careful you don't pull the trigger. Its name is Springstrike, it's very special.'

Ba Ba grunted. 'Haven't seen that in a long time.'

'It's beautiful,' Mei said. It was red lacquered wood, carved with cranes and plum blossoms, with gold caps on the ends of the shaft. Mei handed the weapon back. 'This is a side of you I've never seen.'

'It's a side that doesn't exist any more,' Ma Ma said, and the crossbow disappeared. 'I just want to live a quiet life with all of you, but however much I try to avoid it, my past chases me down and hurts those around me.'

'That's not important,' Ba Ba said. 'Family is what's important.'

'Ba Ba's right,' Di Di said. 'And we're here, and safe, and all together, and free from that awful demon. Everything will be all right.'

Mei sighed with bliss and watched the Shen playing above them. 'I know.'

Ba Ba's head nodded by the time they'd finished the fifth course of the celebratory feast the Palace servants had made for them.

'Go to bed, Ba Ba,' Mei said.

'Come on, Old Bean, I'll take you,' Ma Ma said, putting her hand out for him to take.

'Go, Mr Lee,' Smallcat said. 'You need to rest.'

'More like I've had too much excellent Sichuan food,' Ba Ba said. He raised Ma Ma's hand. 'Come on, wife, I'll tuck you in.'

'Don't you young people stay up too late, we need plan what we'll do when we get back home tomorrow,' Ma Ma said.

After her parents had gone, Mei, Smallcat and Di Di shared a pot of truly excellent Shui Xin tea in the villa's living room.

'So tell us what happened?' Mei asked Di Di. 'How did they get you?'

'I was late closing up the clinic,' Di Di said.

'Clinic?' Smallcat said, interrupting him. 'You're a doctor?'

'Vet,' Di Di said. 'Well, nearly. I was in my final year at the university, doing work experience in a clinic in Sai Kung.'

'Do you think you could have a look at my right front paw?' Smallcat said, sitting straighter. 'My right hand is fine, but in cat form I have shooting pains down the front of my leg into my paw and ...' His voice trailed off. 'Sorry. Please continue.'

Di Di cocked his head to one side. 'Cat? You called the White Tiger "Dad".'

'Forest cat,' Smallcat said.

'A rarity! I'd love to see, what colour are you? What's your fur like? Change and I'll have a look at your foot,' Di Di said.

'No, it can wait. Tell your sister what happened,' Smallcat said.

'Yes!' Mei said.

'Oh. Yeah. Anyway. I was late closing the clinic and they were waiting for me. A really big demon that looked like a fifteen-year-old schoolgirl, with a couple of huge demon guards. They took me down the alley behind the clinic...' He winced. 'She said that Tony loved you, and he wanted to marry you, but he had to make sure you'd say yes and stay with him, so he was planning to blackmail you – with me. I was about to change to fox form and tear their throats out ... ' He shrugged. 'I came around in the hospital and "Holy shit that's the White Tiger Shen, right in front of my little red nose".'

'He played us from start to finish,' Mei said with misery.

'Now do you understand? Never mess with demons!' Smallcat said.

'I get it, I understand, never again,' Mei said. 'So: we have six million US dollars. Ma Ma and Ba Ba can retire if they like, but you and me should keep working. You need to go back and finish your degree. I can return to being an accountant, but I don't know how we'll get you back into university...' Mei said.

'I can arrange that,' Smallcat said. 'The Shen of Heaven have quite a lot of influence on the Earthly Plane. We can do it.'

Di Di smiled with relief.

'This may work out after all,' Mei said.

There was a tap on the villa's front door and Smallcat's eyes unfocussed. 'It's Dad.'

'Tell him I won't marry him and to go away,' Mei said.

'My sister is finally growing some good sense,' Di Di said with amusement. 'You marry that bastard and I will never speak to you again.'

'I said I knew you weren't ready for a relationship,' the Tiger said as he came in. He acknowledged Smallcat's salute with a nod. 'I'm here to offer you a job.'

'Doing what?' Mei said suspiciously.

'What you intended. Helping the prostitutes.'

'Helping prostitutes?' Di Di said with horror.

'Shut up, Leung, they were doing what they had to, to protect and provide for their families,' Mei said. 'Tony had them locked into one-sided contracts and threatened their families if they tried to leave. I was planning to free them.'

'I already did free them, but I want you to do what you planned. Help them gain an education, and a worthwhile career,' the Tiger said. 'I want you to run things for me.'

'How much will you pay me?' Mei said. 'Will I be based outside Hong Kong, away from my family?'

'I'll pay you whatever's the normal pay for a top chief executive officer,' the Tiger said. 'You can be based in Hong Kong and travel around the region; how about I give you a secretary who can teleport you?'

'This sounds too good to be true,' Mei said, still suspicious.

'Take the job, Mei,' Smallcat said out of the corner of his mouth.

'Who'll be teleporting her?' Di Di said, just as suspicious.

'Of course, me,' Smallcat said. 'I don't have much use here in the Western Palace except for minor clerical work, I'm not a warrior, and being Mei's secretary would be very rewarding. I'd love to do it.'

'Did you two work this out together?' Mei said, looking from the Tiger to Smallcat.

'Well that's obvious,' Di Di said. 'I think you should do it, Mei, you'd be great. We know you can trust Shen to do the right thing.'

'One condition,' Mei said, and both the Tiger and Smallcat lit up.

'What?' the Tiger said, his face full of delight.

'You can't ask me on a date. You can't ask me to marry you. You can't court me at all. If I decide to have a relationship with you, I will start it and I will have it on my own terms and you have absolutely no say in the matter.'

The Tiger let his breath out. 'Wah. I've pursued hundreds of women over the centuries and not a single one has ever said anything remotely like that to me before.'

'Please say yes, Dad,' Smallcat said. 'I want more than anything to work with her, she rocks!' He winked at Mei. 'Nobody has ever so comprehensively put my father in his place.'

'Your word?' Mei said.

'My word,' the Tiger said. 'Your terms, your choice, your time.'

'Very well, I accept,' Mei said. 'Let's talk about the terms of reference for this position.'

'Can you look at my paw, now, Leung?' Smallcat said.

'You two go and talk a walk in the gardens and share grooming tips,' Mei said. 'I'll stay here and talk with my *friend*.'

'I am mortally wounded,' the Tiger said, his tawny eyes full of delight.

Di Di and Smallcat shared a look and they both smiled. Mei sighed as they went out the door together into the moonlight.

'Now tell me about this job,' Mei said to the Tiger.

'Don't you want to hear about how I single-handedly went into a demon nest and –'

'No,' she said, cutting him off. 'Professional courtesy, Mr Bai. Tell me about the job and I'll start as soon as I've settled my family back home and have my brother safely returned to his university course.'

118

'You know what?' the Tiger said, leaning his chin on his hand and eyeing her. 'You're far too special to be one of a hundred, you should be the only wife, treasured for the exceptional woman you are.'

'Terms of reference, Mr Bai,' Mei said.

'I have a couple of sons who are smart and brave and of course, extremely good looking...' the Tiger began.

Mei rose to go out.

'No! No! I don't mean it! Sit. Sit!' he said, desperate. 'I won't try to set you up. Your terms. Suit yourself, Miss Lee.'

She sat again. 'Good. Now tell me what stage you're at with the women who used to work for Tony.'

'They're in an integrated chip manufacturing plant in Shenzhen, that was cleared out when we destroyed the demon owner ...' the Tiger began.

Mei smiled as she listened. She was free now, to choose to love whoever she wanted. And she was damn sure she would take her time about making that choice.

Extract From
KYLIE CHAN'S DARK HEAVENS
BOOK ONE
WHITE TIGER

'Mother, Leo,' Simone whispered.

'Oh my God,' Leo said under his breath.

I readied myself and hefted my sword. 'I'm right behind you.'

'Stay there. Don't get in the way. If I go down ...' He hesitated. 'Don't let it have you, Emma. It won't hurt her, she'll be okay. But whatever you do, don't let it take you.'

'I understand.'

The demon appeared in the doorway.

Its back end was a slimy snake that oozed toxin over its black scales. The front end looked like the top half of a man with the skin taken off. It had to lower itself onto its coils to fit through the door; it was enormous.

It came halfway into the room and raised its body on the coils. Its skinless head nearly touched the ceiling. 'You are the Black Lion? Disciple of the Dark Lord?'

'I am just an ordinary man.'

The demon smiled and its red eyes flashed. 'I like your skin. I think I will take it.'

Leo readied himself. 'Come and get it.'

Find more about Kylie's books at her website: www.kyliechan.com

CPSIA information can be obtained
at www.ICGtesting.com
Printed in the USA
FFOW04n0611020317